Gregory

Hathaway House, Book 7

Dale Mayer

Books in This Series:

GREGORY: HATHAWAY HOUSE, BOOK 7
Dale Mayer
Valley Publishing Ltd.

Copyright © 2019

ISBN-13: 978-1-773362-79-3
Print Edition

About This Book

Welcome to Hathaway House, a heartwarming and sweet military romance series from USA TODAY best-selling author Dale Mayer. Here you'll meet a whole new group of friends, along with a few favorite characters from Heroes for Hire. Instead of action, you'll find emotion. Instead of suspense, you'll find healing. Instead of romance, ... oh, wait. ... There is romance—of course!

Welcome to Hathaway House. Rehab Center. Safe Haven. Second chance at life and love.

Navy SEAL Gregory Parkins knows he's not so bad off as to need what Hathaway House offers, but he'll do anything to get in. RN Meredith Anderson is there, and Greg loves Meredith. In the time since they split up, his life has been one disaster after another, including the one that ended his career—the career that separated them in the first place.

Meredith was horrified to hear what happened to Gregory. But seeing his file was an even bigger shock. Greg thinks he's basically back to normal, but Meredith knows he has a long way to go. She doesn't know how to tell him, without running the risk of him leaving Hathaway House before his healing can really take place.

But the last thing she wants is for him to walk away from her again. Not if there is any chance that they can find their way back to each other ...

Prologue

GREGORY PARKINS STARED at the application in his hand and wondered. He'd had this thing printed off and filled out half a dozen times in the last couple weeks, and every time he had balled it up and threw it away. Hathaway House was just one of many other rehab centers that he had thought of going to. He knew he needed to go to this one though, but it wasn't so much for himself but because of the woman he had left behind.

He wouldn't have had a clue that she was even there if not for a write-up about Hathaway House that had hit the internet and gone viral. Something about Dani and her father and what they had accomplished since they built the center. The article had piqued his interest, and he'd gone looking to see what kind of a rehab center it was. His research had led him to photographs of the staff at the center, and there, sure enough, he'd seen the photo that had sent him into a tailspin.

Meredith, the woman he had left behind the last time he had headed off on a mission. It had already been five years, but he'd never forgotten her. Gregory could only hope that she'd never forgotten him either. But the chances were, she'd moved on, was likely married and had a family by now.

But he didn't know that. Should he reach out to her or just ignore this? *Ignore?* His laugh was hollow, completely devoid of emotions. He knew he couldn't ignore her. Wasn't that evident by the number of times he'd filled out the paper applications only to crumple them up and throw them away? He and Meredith had spent three wonderful weeks together, and he thought he'd found *the one*.

When he had finally told her that he was leaving again, she'd been heartbroken. Desolate. Her brother had died overseas, and she didn't want to deal with the same kind of loss again. Gregory understood, but he'd signed up for the navy as soon as he could, right out of school. He'd been honored to join, and his career had fulfilled him every year since. No way would he walk away at that point.

As soon as he left her, he regretted his decision.

He knew he should have turned around and found a way to make this work, but instead, he'd buried himself in his work and had tried to forget her. And, for a time, he'd managed. But then he had been blown up by an IED. Now, if he went to look for her, he would feel like *he* was second-best, like he had only come back to her because he was no longer whole. No longer fit for the navy, so she was his second choice.

Again.

Just like before.

But for different reasons.

He didn't want that. Nor did he want her to feel that way.

Yet, if she was still at the rehab center and single, they had a chance to work on a whole new level of a relationship. And with so many more problems than they had originally. Even to him, that sounded harsh, but the truth was often harsh. He didn't even know why she would want him back in this state. He'd be offering her less than what he had been before, and yet, he'd walked away from her.

He snorted.

As if he were fully capable of walking away anymore. Because he no longer could. ... Not without crutches, a wheelchair or a prosthetic.

Gregory laid the paperwork off to the side. He had also filled out the online form but hadn't really worked on the last couple questions, determined to at least do that much as he knew Hathaway House could help him physically if nothing else. Maybe he could walk away from Meredith again and not regret it this time. Maybe, just maybe, he could find a whole new life. Sometimes one had to go through the pain to get to the closure, and eventually, to reach a new life at the other end.

He quickly filled out the last few questions online; then his gaze landed on Meredith's picture once more. Not giving himself much chance to rethink anything, he reviewed the online application—the same as the physical paperwork he had filled out a dozen times—and hit Send.

For better or for worse, his application was in.

Chapter 1

MEREDITH ANDERSON STOOD at the reception desk as she watched her colleague flip through the stacks of incoming patients. "How many today?"

"Three," Melissa said. "I can't believe it. We've had such a high turnover lately."

"Yes, but a good high turnover," Meredith replied. "Every patient's gone home in much better shape than they arrived. It's not a case of them leaving because they aren't happy or leaving because they, ... you know, ... passed away," she said. "They're leaving because they can go home in better shape than when they first got here."

"I know," Melissa said, a beautiful smile breaking across her face. "It's awesome. But, at the same time, that's three new people today alone. We need more nurses if this keeps up." She handed off the files for Meredith's review and said, "I think they're all coming in this afternoon."

Meredith shook her head. "And we need more doctors and therapists too, and poor Dani needs at least one full-time assistant. Plus, Stan could use another veterinarian as well. I know he's waiting on Aaron to complete his studies, but maybe they can hire a temporary vet in the meantime?"

"Dani's interviewing now for some position. Not sure for what position but you know she won't hire someone to help her until the rest of us have more help."

"So true. One of us may have to hire someone behind her back," Meredith whispered with a sly grin.

"As if Dani doesn't know everything that's going on here," Melissa said, grinning too. "But there's always the major. He could get that done." Melissa winked.

"Good idea. We should approach him on that matter the next time we see him alone—or at least not with Dani." Meredith sighed. "Back to the work at hand." She looked at the first new patient intake file and noted that this guy was fifty-seven years old, with two damaged hips and both knees gone. She winced. "Ouch, Bob." She flipped to the second new patient's file. This one was a much younger man, yet he had severe back injuries—which was not unusual here. Hathaway House worked miracles with patients thought to be permanently damaged and beyond improvement.

The third new patient's file came with an even greater shock. This one had a missing foot and half his lower leg and a forearm that had a recent surgery.

She found an unopened envelope added to the file. It contained a further typed update from the surgeon, stating how he was cautiously optimistic after the last surgical procedure, would have liked to have had the patient under his care for six more weeks, but that the patient was determined to make this switch in order to take advantage of an empty bed here. The doctor's handwritten note at the bottom added that the patient's mental outlook was just as important as his physical outlook, so the doctor felt good about this patient's decision. Would love to hear from his new surgeons as to Gregory's six-week checkup. *Hmmm.*

Also, this patient was missing a couple ribs and had some steel plates inserted. She whistled when she took a look at the X-ray of the steel plates and then a few photos of his back, both pre-op and post-op. "Wow, I bet you met up with an IED and not in a good way," she whispered. She flipped through the thick file, shaking her head at the damage noted in his records and confirmed by more before and after photos of his chest and his arms and legs included too, then looked at the patient's name.

Gregory Parkins.

Her heart stalled.

She picked up the file, walked around the corner to Dani's office and asked, "Dani, do you know this guy?"

Dani looked up, saw the folder in Meredith's hand and asked, "What's the name?"

"Gregory," she said. "Gregory ... Parkins."

"No. He's one of the new patient intakes, isn't he?" Dani asked, before settling in her chair, leaning back, and instantly recognizing the look on Meredith's face. "What is it?"

"I knew him five years ago," Meredith said, rooted in place.

"Oh my," Dani said, as she bounced to her feet. "Like *knew* him?"

"The love of my life," Meredith said drily. "At least for three glorious weeks."

Dani let out a peal of laughter. "Oh my," she said again. "Well, I'm glad you had those three weeks."

"Yes. ... And no. ... I didn't want him to go back to the navy, but he went anyway." Meredith was near tears and felt so stupid. She thought she had dealt with this. Over and over and over again. She reminded herself that this was five years ago. *Five.* Why couldn't she forget Gregory? It was *only* three weeks of her life. ... She swallowed, shook her head, trying to not cry in front of Dani.

Dani frowned, walked toward her friend. "One of the hardest lessons anybody has to learn when dealing with military men," Dani said, "is to realize that these men go into the navy or the air force or whatever because they have a deep abiding passion for it. They have already made the heart-heavy decision to leave family and friends and loved ones to take on that lifestyle. And not just for one hitch or one tour. It's in their blood or deep in their soul or resident in their very DNA. They have to follow that drive, that pull, or they are never happy themselves. It's almost impossible for them to walk away from the military call."

"Oh, I realized that afterward," Meredith said. "*Immediately* afterward, … yet I was too late.'

Dani patted her friend on the shoulder. "And," Dani continued, "it takes a special woman to pair up with these men. As a nurse, you are more qualified than most to deal with their war wounds, both physical and mental." She saw the pained look on Meredith's face. "But dealing with the long and constant separations are another matter entirely. Nursing school probably doesn't cover that issue. … Sit down, Meredith," she said softly, leading her dumbstruck friend into a nearby chair.

"When I couldn't find *any* other man to *even begin* to replace him, I … I realized that a little bit of him was a whole lot better than none of him."

Dani nodded in understanding. "Long-distance relationships are not for everybody. To only see your partner when they're back home every once in a while …" She shook her head. "Some women can handle six months of single life at a time, even when married on paper. I'm dealing with being engaged, and yet, separated from my fiancé now while Aaron is in school and not living here at Hathaway House or even in town. And I'm okay with that. For the most part. *For now.* For a couple years of his hard work at school, while I suffer through those couple years of me dealing with the absence of him, then we can be together twenty-four seven for three hundred and sixty-five days of every year thereafter."

Dani laughed. "There are times I don't think I can do this, but … but you have to understand your own tolerances for this setup. Like wives whose husbands worked on the pipeline or even now work on those Gulf Coast offshore rigs. I hear they are on one week and off the next, or some work two weeks on-site and are off two weeks. That doesn't compare to the military's tours, which are so far away and for much longer stretches of time. But regardless it's a different lifestyle, and both parties have to be okay with it for those relationships to work." Dani sat next to Meredith and rubbed her arm. "But now you get to meet Gregory again."

"Yeah," Meredith said, holding up his thick file folder. "His body has been destroyed."

"Yes," Dani said. "I remember that case. The question really is, can you handle working with him, or would you like me to assign him to somebody else?"

"I'll handle it," she said. "Just like I handle every other patient." Meredith took a deep inhale, letting it out slowly. "But to read what's happened to him …" Meredith shook her head, words failing her. She looked at Dani and winced. "Why do I feel so guilty? Why am I … so very mad? Why am I feeling such frustration and helplessness? … Why am I even telling you all this right after I just said I could handle this?"

"Like what drove Gregory to serve, you have a drive within you that makes you a great nurse. You have empathy for your patients. It may be in overdrive with Gregory, but I understand. Totally. And maybe it's a good thing that you have seen this now," she said, "so that, when you do see him for the first time, you won't be shocked, and you won't let him down by crying." She noted Meredith's trembling lower lip.

"This is so hard," Meredith whispered. "I loved him so very much."

"Well, I'm a great believer in true love lasting forever," she said. "So, if you loved him, maybe that love is still there."

"Maybe. ... Maybe I still do love him even now. Maybe that's why I can't just close that chapter of my life, why I have remembered him at the most random times over these last five years," Meredith said sadly. "But he walked away from me, so what kind of love is that?"

"Was he as devastated as you were to leave you behind?"

Meredith shook her head. "He wasn't glib about it, if that's what you mean."

Dani smiled softly. "He was in pain?"

"I thought so," Meredith whined, wiping the tears in her eyes.

"So the big tough guy was hiding his feelings?"

"Probably. At least I hope so." Meredith hiccupped.

"And you never heard from him again?"

"Not one word."

"Yet you said you still thought about him, didn't you?"

Meredith nodded, her head down.

"So maybe the big tough navy guy thought about you too, over the years."

Meredith shrugged, still not making eye contact with Dani.

Dani paused, giving Meredith a moment to catch her

composure.

Meredith straightened in the chair, sniffled, raised her head to glare at Dani and repeated her question. "But he walked away from me, so what kind of love is that?"

"The kind of love that you can't argue with," Dani said. "Your love doesn't necessarily have to be the same love that anybody else has. Love is individual. It's unique to all of us and to each relationship. The trick to it is making it yours, whatever version it is."

"I wish you'd been around five years ago," Meredith said, slumping in her chair. "Because that would have helped me a lot."

"Wouldn't it?" Dani said. "But I had my own demons to deal with too. You must work your way through this. Just give it time."

"I thought I did. I thought I already had. I survived five years without him. That should have been enough. That should have been plenty. But it wasn't. I thought that was hard. And now I have to get myself together in a handful of hours before he pops into my life again. What I dealt with for five years doesn't begin to compare with *this*." She raised Gregory's heavy file in the air and shook it. "And now I can't let him know how affected I am by his physical condition?" she asked.

"Yes," Dani said. "As a medical professional—and as his friend—the biggest thing is to never show pity. Especially for these men, but all men in general, what with their egos and that protector mindset and the provider image they all seem born with. But particularly when dealing with these military types, wounded or not. Never let Gregory think that you consider him less of a man than he was before."

GREGORY SLOWLY MADE his way up the ramp on crutches, an orderly helping on either side. He knew he was being beyond stubborn, and his latest surgeon would be swearing mad to see this, and Gregory knew he was probably pushing his luck, but it seemed wrong to be wheeled over the threshold to this next stage of his life. He wanted to face it head-on. He also knew that chances were, the crutches weren't the right thing to do. It was too early yet. Too soon after the latest surgery on his arm. Which was iffy yet. Too soon after the added exertion of traveling.

As he stood in the reception area, trembling but vertical, he could see one of the orderlies motioning to somebody just out of his view. Next thing Gregory knew, a wheelchair backed up to him. The orderly leaned down and said, "Sit." Gregory recognized the order inherent in that soft word. Shaky and needing a hand, he managed to sit in the wheelchair, desperately trying not to show how relieved he was to get off his foot and relieving the stress off his back and arm.

A woman stepped from an office nearby and smiled at him. "Welcome to Hathaway House," she said. "I'm Dani, owner and manager."

He smiled and shook her hand. "I'm glad to be here," he said honestly. "I was pretty surprised when I was accepted."

"We accept a lot of people from all walks of life and with all kinds of injuries."

He nodded but didn't say anything.

She motioned to the orderly beside him and said, "Gregory's assigned to 242."

The orderly nodded, and together the three of them proceeded down one of the many hallways off the main reception area, while Dani explained the workings of Hathaway House. It looked pretty normal to Gregory, a hallway with lots of doors, people in wheelchairs and people on crutches. Nothing special at all.

She pointed to a door up ahead and said, "This one's yours." She opened it wide, and he went in.

Pleasantly surprised, he realized he had a private room with a window and almost like a balcony, if he could get out there to enjoy it. A bed and a bath. He nodded and said, "Well, this is nice."

She chuckled. "How to damn with faint praise."

He flushed at that. "Sorry," he said. "I was just thinking that, as I came down the hallway, it seemed very much like every other center I've been in."

The orderly behind him laughed. "There's nothing ordinary about this place," he said. "Yes, it looks like bedroom upon bedroom, and yes, you'll see an awful lot of similar-looking patients. But that's where the resemblance ends."

Dani dropped a stack of paperwork and a tablet on his bed. "Most of that is self-explanatory," she said. "But, because of what you just said, let's take a quick walk around, and you can see what you get to look forward to."

They wheeled him back out into the hallway and down a few more doors and turned a corner, and then everything opened up. He was surprised—again—when they kept on going into a big entertainment section. Even though it was midafternoon or so, people were gathered here, noisily playing pool and various other board games, like checkers and chess, along with maybe poker at one table and other card games at a couple more. He had to smirk when he saw a jigsaw puzzle spread nearby across a bigger table, and already a couple men were seated there, quietly immersed in the activity, ignoring the hoots and hollers from the tables next to them.

But what called to Gregory more was an outdoor deck area, with its railing providing a panoramic view of probably three sides of this property. When they got closer to another glass double-wide doorway, the entrance opened up to a large cafeteria. All the while, the orderly kept on rambling about different things, such as when mealtimes were, ... food always available anytime he was hungry, day or night, so he was to come and get something. ... Coffee always fresh, ... juices and fruits, ... water.

Gregory didn't pay much attention to it. He was keenly taking in the layout with interest. When Dani led him to the railing side so he could look down and see the horses in the fields and the pool beneath him, Gregory found himself truly smiling for the very first time since he had gotten here. "Now this is more like it," he said.

She looked at him. "You like horses?"

"Yep, used to rodeo when I was a kid."

She chuckled, making Gregory's smile widen. "Well," she said, "I do have a couple horses that we use for riding sometimes. So anytime you want to or think you're strong enough to get on the back of one again, those requests go through me. But we'll also need your therapist's and doctor's permissions. Still, it's definitely something you can look forward to," she concluded.

"Thank you. I'd like that," he said sincerely.

"But no rodeoing," she added as if on second thought. "However, I'm happy to take you on a quarter horse and go out in the pastures for an hour or two, as soon as you're strong enough."

"Great. What about the pool?"

"As soon as you're cleared, you get pool time."

"Well then, I'd like to get through the therapists, the doctors and the testing as soon as possible," he said, "because I'm half fish, and I've really, really missed the water."

"Spoken like a true Navy SEAL." The woman had a gentle smile on her lips as she spoke. It made her seem even warmer and more welcoming than before.

Gregory was watching her motion with her left hand as she kept on speaking until she stopped and walked up to a big barreled-chested man, sitting comfortably in a wheelchair—or as comfortable as one could sit with stumps where his legs should be. Both of them were bandaged, and he held something in his beefy arms so small that Gregory couldn't see what it was from where he sat. Dani reached down and scooped it up, then, coming back to him, she resumed talking.

"We have a veterinary clinic below us. They perform the normal functions of an animal clinic. However, they serve a double duty for us as we also run a lot of shelter animals through here, and we have multiple therapy animals in-house too."

At this point, Gregory realized what the man had been holding. It was the tiniest little dog he had ever seen, and Dani held it out to him.

"This is Chickie. Don't ever feed him because he's missing most of his stomach and doesn't digest food very well. But he's got a huge fan following in the place."

Gregory reached out and gently cuddled the tiniest, most broken-looking Chihuahua he'd ever seen in his life. He drew him up to his face to give him a kiss. It's huge eyes and little tongue licked at Gregory's mouth and chin and broke his heart.

"Wow, how many therapy animals are here?" Just then a very large Maine coon cat hopped up into his lap and purred, batting at his hand. He was so surprised to have the cat and Chickie in his arms that he stared in amazement, but his free hand immediately stroked the beautiful gray cat.

"That's Thomas," she said. "Helga's around here too. She's a Newfoundlander dog with three legs. You'll see Thomas there is missing a back leg too."

"Doesn't seem to affect his jumping though," Gregory noted.

"No, if anything, he uses it to get more food and cuddles out of everybody," she said in a dry tone. "A baby llama is over there"—Dani pointed out to a nearby field—"Her name is Lovely. The horse at her side—they're a bonded pair—is called Appie. They were both removed from their owner for abuse. Appie's hooves were almost curled over they were so long, and he was starved. Lovely was in the same condition, but thankfully both of them have recovered quite nicely. We have a filly here too. We also have my horses, which are my own personal mounts, and my home is adjacent to the center." She pointed again as she spoke. "We have more dogs, and we have a goat." She laughed. "If you like animals, you're in the right place."

"I love animals," Gregory said. Chickie, as if understanding, curled up ever-so-slightly into the crook of his elbow and looked to be going to sleep while Thomas curled up on his lap, prepared to stay there. He stared at them in amazement. "Seriously, I love all animals. So can they go back to my room too?"

"They can go with you back to your room, but you have to leave your door open, so they can come and go at will," she answered him. "Independence and freedom for our people and our animals is paramount here. Thomas has litter boxes throughout our center, and Chickie, while carried about mostly, has a special bed up at the front reception area. Racer, another of our therapy animals, has a set of wheels that come off and on, but they allow him to race around the hallways. So leave your door open if you have any animals, so they're never forcibly kept in your room. As soon as that happens, it's a strike against you, and you won't be allowed to keep the animals at all."

"Freedom," he said, "it's so important to everyone."

"So is independence," Dani responded with a smile. "And they have that here in spades. Don't feed *any* of the animals. Most of them are on special diets. We do have a full-time vet downstairs. You'll meet him soon enough," she said. "And, if you ever want to visit some of the animals downstairs, we have an elevator that can get you down there. There are also stairs and a ramp, depending on what skill level you're currently at. You're welcome to go down there at any time. They often have animals that just need some love. From foster animals to rescue animals that are in for surgery from all kinds of incidents, you're welcome to visit."

He could feel his heart expanding with joy just even holding little Chickie against his heart. "Wow," he whispered, lifting the little guy up again and kissing the top of his head. "These guys have got to be one of the biggest blessings to your place."

"Oh? But not the pool?" Dani laughed.

"Well, that's a big help too," Gregory said with a smile. "So, how do I get started?"

"Well, it's four p.m., so you get to start today by going over the paperwork. We have some signatures required." She led the way back to his room. "The tablet has your schedule keyed in, and it also has a list of your medical team members. You've been assigned a primary doctor and three secondary doctors, plus a primary care nurse, a therapist, and half a dozen other people in your team," she said with a wave of her hand. "All of their bios are listed, so you can see who they are and what they specialize in. They each will interview you. Once they are done with that, they will get together and create a special treatment program for you here."

"Okay, thank you."

"No problem. You won't see two of the doctors right now though. I believe one is in town doing surgery, but he'll be back later tonight. So you could have people from your team stopping by your room up to eight p.m. tonight. We do try to prevent people from going to your room after eight on any given night. ... That is, except for the night-shift nurses."

"Right. I think my medical records made it here already, didn't they?"

"They did, indeed." They were already back in his room. "You'll find a robe and some towels, so you can shower whenever you are ready. Your personal belongings are here too." She pointed to his bag. "We don't unpack for our residents. We feel that helps you acclimate quicker if you know where your personal effects are. However, if at any time you need help, please don't hesitate to ask. We especially don't want to overtax you or stress you further after your travels to get here to us today. And dinnertime is around an hour from now."

"But I can eat even though I haven't met the rest of the team?" he asked hopefully.

"Yes, that's correct. Just the more of your team you can see today and tomorrow, the better. Your rehab program can't really start until you've met everybody on your team. So make yourself available as much as you can."

"May I bring food back to my room?" he asked, wondering just how strict the rules here were.

"You are welcome to eat in your room, but I'd suggest doing that in about an hour or so, whether here or in the cafeteria. Now that you've arrived, a notice has gone out to everybody on your team, so you're likely to get inundated by them in the next hour," she replied. "Therefore, I suggest you wait until at least five-thirty p.m. to visit the cafeteria. I'll input a note, saying that you're heading in for food after that time."

"Okay, good."

Dani handed him the paperwork and the tablet and showed him that he had a call button to contact her or the nurses in case of any issues.

And then she was gone.

Chapter 2

MEREDITH HATED THE fact that she was nervous. Yet she gave herself some kudos for doing as well as she was, given her seven-hour notice to deal with a pretty major surprise in her life. Shaking that thought off, she set aside her personal issues and donned her professional hat, so to speak. She knew she needed to see Gregory. She was his primary care nurse, she kept reminding herself. She'd stopped by once, but one of his doctors had already been in there with Gregory. She'd immediately taken that as an excuse to walk on by.

But she couldn't put it off for long, regardless of how many other people were on his team. They all needed to see Gregory to do their jobs properly. And, with Gregory's current extensive physical problems, they all had to meet with him immediately to get his rehab started. She sighed. She'd see him, doing her best to be there for him, but she'd rather do it before dinner and get that initial meet-and-greet behind her. Then maybe she could relax some. Put some of her fears aside. She quickly snagged her files and the tablet and walked toward his room. She could feel her heart shaking and her fingers sweating. She hated that. Absolutely hated that.

Dani's words echoed in her mind. *Don't show him pity.*

Meredith definitely wouldn't do that, but she was already having trouble dealing with his battered body because she knew how broken he was; his medical file had been quite comprehensive. When she compared that to how he'd been before and how much pain he'd been through in the interim, her heart broke every time she thought about it because she should have been there with him. There *for* him. But he hadn't let her.

No, that's not true. They hadn't even given themselves the chance to take that step. They hadn't given themselves the chance to even have that kind of an opportunity, to see if they could have had a real relationship. Once he'd said he was going back, she got angry, and that had been it.

She knocked on his door. It was open a couple inches, but she wasn't sure if he was alone.

"Come in."

Taking a deep breath, she pushed open the door and walked in as if nothing was different. She smiled up at him and said, "Hi, welcome to Hathaway House." She had to stop herself from instinctively hugging Gregory.

Gregory looked at her and muttered, "Hi," but he didn't show any signs of recognition.

She tilted her head to the side and introduced herself. "I'm Meredith."

He nodded slowly. "I remember," he said, but his tone was indifferent, like he was talking about the weather or something.

Meredith's heart sank, but she schooled her expression. At least she hoped she did. *So no hugs needed or wanted by* this *Gregory.* Giving a polite nod, she replied, "Good, I hope the time we had together has been forgotten."

He tilted his head ever-so-slightly. "Meaning?"

She took a deep breath and said, "Just that we were

friends once, and I don't want our prior relationship to hold back your healing."

Instantly, he dropped his gaze, and then he smiled and said, "Thank you for that. I have no intention of letting that happen."

Not quite the response that she wanted but okay. *I'm his primary care nurse.* She returned his smile. "I'll be your primary care nurse, as I was assigned to your medical team. I don't know if you've seen everybody else yet on your team," she said, "but obviously I have a little more history with you than probably the other members."

"You might have known me before," he said with a curt nod, "but the last five years have seen a lot of changes."

"Obviously, and not for the better, and for that I'm sorry," she said sincerely. "Sometimes life can be a bear."

He gave a hard laugh at that. "That's one way to call it."

She motioned toward the door. "It's almost five-thirty, and we have a notation here that you wanted to eat then. Do you want to come with me so I can show you the ropes?"

Gregory hesitated.

Immediately she backed up and said, "Got it. If you need me for anything, just hit the Call button." And, with that, she disappeared.

"OUCH," GREGORY MUTTERED. "Couldn't have made that any worse if I'd tried."

He should have called her back, and he probably still could, but it would be a bit awkward now. He should have just done it, so why hadn't he?

He stared at the tablet in front of him and realized he

could call her back. Once again forcing himself to do what didn't come naturally, he pushed the button and then sat here and waited. When she came around the doorway, a puzzled frown on her face, he just stared at her.

She shook her head, looked at him and asked, "What's up?"

"If you hadn't run away quite so fast," he said, "I could have explained. I would like to go to the cafeteria. ... Yes, I would like you to show me the ropes. But I need to make a trip to the washroom first, and that can take me a little time." He watched as a smile bloomed across her face.

"Well then, why don't you do that now? I have to step into my office anyway, and I'll be back in a few minutes." And then, just like the first time, she disappeared.

Gregory took a deep breath and slowly let it out. He just needed to process a little faster. Everything in his life seemed to have slowed down since sustaining his injuries. It's not that he'd had a brain trauma, but he didn't seem to have the lightning-quick mentality that he'd had before. He didn't know if it was something from the initial injury itself or just another side effect due to these big changes in his life's circumstances.

Regardless, she had given him a second chance, and, if he could at least put them on a friendly basis, then she was right. It wouldn't slow down his healing. Meredith had had a lovely personality before—hopefully she still did. It was that in particular which had attracted him to her, her fresh openness to everything and to everyone.

He'd always admired her, her bubbliness, her offer of friendship that had been so welcome back then. He didn't want to lose it now if she was offering it a second time. Whether it would come to anything more, he didn't know, but he didn't want to take the chance of it being here and him being too proud to pick up what was offered. He had a lot of issues, and pride was one of them. So was stubbornness. But the biggest issue right now was to see if anything still remained between them.

She was lovely as always. Inside and out.

Unlike him. He stared down at his broken body and shook his head, then maneuvered himself to the edge of the bed, and, with his crutches, he slowly made his way to the bathroom, albeit very shakily. When he was done, he was done in more ways than one. As much as he wanted to go to the cafeteria under his own steam, he would have to use the wheelchair tonight. Back out of the bathroom again, he slowly made his way to the wheelchair, clumsily collapsing into it.

Catching his breath, he carefully laid the crutches across the bed. One of the biggest challenges was having what he needed available when he wanted it. Like his crutches. He needed to have them on hand, and invariably they were just out of reach. He would see about getting a sling to carry them on the back of his wheelchair or whatever was the current update for that. He wouldn't need either for long. At least not full-time. He had high hopes for a prosthetic and knew that was possible here at Hathaway House.

Finally, he wheeled his way slowly to the doorway of his room and looked around the corner, and there she was, walking toward him.

A smile lit up her face. "Hungry?"

Gregory didn't answer immediately. He sank back into his chair, realizing that, for the first time in a very long time, he might actually get through this. Meaning, reconnecting with her and getting his body as healed as was possible. He smiled back at her. "Absolutely. I'm starved."

With that, he slowly turned the wheelchair down the hallway, hoping she wouldn't offer him any assistance. There were only so many dents to his pride that a man could take. But she walked at his side quite comfortably as he slowly maneuvered his chair. He appreciated her slower pace, so that he wasn't pushed into rushing. He didn't think he could handle that right now. Then again, she was probably used to being around people like him. She dealt with broken men all the time.

Chapter 3

A S FAR AS Meredith was concerned, this was one of the strangest feelings she'd had. It was as if not only had time had disappeared so that they were once again walking together but also had disappeared in a way that neither was acknowledging.

They hadn't left on the best of circumstances, and yet, they were also not meeting in the best of circumstances, and they were both ignoring the great big span of time between those two emotion-filled points. Inside, she didn't quite know what to say or how to act, so, as donning the mantle of professionalism, she gave him information regarding the Hathaway House cafeteria as they walked along. "If ever you're hungry outside of normal mealtimes," she said, "you can contact Dennis at any time. There's also always coffee and muffins and tea and hot water. ... Things like that are available all hours too. And there's a big refrigerator full of juices and dairy products, if you can eat dairy."

"Good to know," he said, his tone noncommittal.

She slid a glance his way, but his gaze busily darted around in all directions but hers. When she noted that, she sighed. "You should be very comfortable here," she said suddenly. "A lot of people are here for similar conditions, a lot of people at various stages of rehab, ... various stages of healing. Most of them have quite the story, but they're all here with one thought in mind, and that's to get better and to go home."

He nodded but didn't add to that.

Sensing the same yawning uncomfortableness between them, Meredith didn't want to walk any faster because he was in his wheelchair. Still, the doors to the cafeteria couldn't come fast enough. "These doors are almost always open. If you see them closed, they are automatic. So, as soon as you put pressure on this"—she stood on the sensor—"they will open."

"That's convenient," he responded.

"When you consider we have people in all states of mobility, it's pretty necessary." When they got to the large area, she said, "There's seating inside and outside. Where would you like to go?"

He pointed to the far back corner, out on the deck. "Depending on how hot the sun is, I wouldn't mind some sunlight," Gregory said. "After being in rehab for so long, that's in short supply. I'm probably completely vitamin D deficient," he joked.

"That sounds good then. Do you need a hand at the cafeteria end?" She tapped his shoulder to point to the other side, and he immediately changed direction.

"I think I can manage. It's similar to what I've had to maneuver through before," he said.

Meredith smiled.

"But hopefully the food here is much better."

She didn't make a comment on that, but she knew that was often a complaint about various centers from the people who transferred in to Hathaway House.

As soon as he got up to the front of the line and saw the food selections, his eyebrows shot up. "Well, it looks good."

He breathed in deeply. "And it smells wonderful."

She got him a tray off the stack and then smiled at Dennis behind the counter. "Dennis, this is Gregory," she said. "He's a new arrival."

"One of several, I hear." Dennis gave a big smile to Gregory and said, "Welcome to Hathaway House. What kind of food do you like?"

"Well, meat and potatoes would work nicely," Gregory joked, smiling up at the big face behind the buffet-style offerings from the kitchen.

Dennis returned his smile. "We've got lots of that here. Chicken, roast beef, fish. … What's your choice?"

"Roast beef," he said. "Does it come with gravy and mashed potatoes?"

"It certainly can," Dennis said. "Do you want green vegetables of any kind?"

Meredith saw Gregory scrunching his nose, like he was obviously contemplating saying no, so she nudged him gently. "Remember. You're here to heal."

Gregory shot her a half-sulky, half-annoyed look, making Dennis laugh heartily.

"How about a side salad?" Dennis offered.

"Not a whole lot of nutrients in a small side salad," Meredith chipped in, totally unfazed by Gregory's look.

VERY QUICKLY GREGORY had a large plate of food in front of him—and, yes, he had steamed green vegetables too. Meredith came behind him, holding her dinner tray. He could see that she had chicken with steamed vegetables and a salad on the side. As they made their way to the other side of the room, Meredith spoke. "You can have coffee now, or you can come back for it later."

"How busy does it get?" he asked, looking around.

"At the wrong time, very busy." She laughed. "We have hundreds of patients and staff here. It's a pretty busy corner of our world. There are lots and lots of seating, but still, the seats will fill rather quickly if we come at rush time."

He nodded. "It doesn't look too bad right now, so maybe I'll risk the coffee a little bit later." With the tray on his lap, he wheeled outside ever-so-slowly, trying to navigate through the tables full of people. He didn't recognize anybody; they all seemed to be seated with friends or staff. Lots of laughter and conversations floated around him.

He made his way to the far side of the deck, where he found an empty table out in the sun. He sat here for a moment with his face up and then realized that he hadn't really asked her if she was eating with him. He turned around, searching for her, and, not seeing her, his heart sank before he saw that she'd stopped to talk to somebody. And, with a wave goodbye, she looked up, saw him waiting for her, nodded and walked toward him.

His own anxiety had brought on that sense of rejection. She should reject him. It would be the right thing to do. After all, he'd rejected her and everything she stood for.

Then she'd done the same thing to him.

He busied himself moving chairs and getting his wheel-chair up to the table and then removed everything from his tray. There was just something about cafeteria-style dining that he hated. He always took his food off the tray, even if it was more work to clean up afterward. It seemed more like a real dining room and not an institutionalized cafeteria if he did it this way.

He sat here, unrolling his cutlery from his cloth napkin, and realized he should have got some water. Glancing back, he noticed it was by the coffee, large glasses poured already. He frowned, considering whether he should make the trip, when Meredith arrived, placed her tray down and said, "I'm going to get water. Do you want a glass?"

"I was just wondering if it was worth making the trip for."

"I'll grab you one," she said and disappeared again.

He should have sat on the other side of the table, so he could look at the people, but he would much rather sit on this side by the railing, where he could look at the acres of green grass and the animals dotting the landscape.

It was a stunning location, plus having the vet down below was beyond interesting. From what Gregory had seen, the animals were a lovely addition, and he knew his own myriad emotions and his heartbeat had calmed considerably when he had met Chickie. And he'd met Thomas the cat but had yet to see Helga—he thought that was her name, but he wasn't sure. A Newfoundlander dog would be hard to miss.

As he stared out across the meadow, waiting for Meredith before he dug in, he saw something black wandering along the fence line. When Meredith returned, giving him a glass of water, he motioned to the fence and said, "Would that be Helga?"

She looked over the rail, nodded and said, "Yes, indeed, it is."

"Do they get to run around on their own like that?"

"They do. The grounds are fenced, so, once they're on that side of it, they can't leave the property, but there are miles of open fields for them to run in and romp around," she admitted. "Still, they're all very attached to their people."

Gregory laughed at that. "I'd love to make a trip down-stairs and see the rest of the clinic."

"You will. You just arrived, so give it time."

"Do I need permission to go down there?"

"No," she said. "Not really. We just need to allow for a little bit of time to make it happen. Overtaxing yourself at the outset is the worst thing you can do. And it happens all too often with new arrivals."

"Right," he said. "I've been told that before."

"Still as stubborn as ever, I presume," she said in a teas-ing voice.

He shrugged and gave her a lopsided grin. "Guilty as charged."

"Well, your team will work on that. Stubbornness is good sometimes. ... It's just not good all the time."

"It's what got me here," he said quietly. "I didn't think I'd ever make it this far."

"Well, I'm glad you were wrong," she said with a gentle smile. "We've seen many success stories here. Some condi-tions get completely turned around in the end. Just because a doctor says something will happen doesn't mean that's what ends up happening. Miracles can and do happen all the time."

"I'm starting to realize that." Gregory stared at her long enough to make her feel uncomfortable, then looked at his food and said, "If this tastes as good as it looks, that's a miracle right here."

At that, she laughed out loud. "Our kitchen's one of the best. We all enjoy the food here. We are constantly com-plaining about getting fat."

He looked at her and raised an eyebrow. "I haven't seen anybody fat yet."

"No, it's not exactly something we encourage, among the staff or the patients," she said. "We do tailor an exercise program when needed, and, if we have to, we can curtail a patient's diet, but we try not to."

"Of course. Most of the people who you have here were active servicemen at some time, weren't they?"

"Yes," she said, "but, on occasion, exceptions have been made to accept civilians as well. Dani has a wide network, and sometimes people call in favors to see if they can get friends and family in, and almost always she does what she can to accommodate them."

"How do you stay active?"

"I like to jog," she admitted. "And I spend a fair bit of time in the pool, usually in the evenings though."

"Does it get busy?" Gregory stared around the railing, down at the far side below, where the pool was, but he couldn't quite see it from where he sat.

"No," she replied. "To accommodate the number of people we can have here at any given time, it is a big pool, but not very many people around the place seem to have an interest in it. Or at least not at any one time, a fact I've always appreciated."

"Of course," Gregory agreed as he tackled his dinner with gusto, stopping about one-third of the way through before speaking again. "Wow, this is really good food."

"It is, isn't it?"

He nodded and then, knowing that he was still dancing around their own issues, asked, "How long have you been here?"

"A few years," she said noncommittally.

He nodded. "So what did you do when I left?"

She took her time answering. "I went back to work at

the same job, but I was struggling, and I desperately wanted a change of scenery, something to help me heal."

Just then Dani walked up to them and interrupted the conversation. She smiled down at Gregory. "Looks like you're settling in just fine." She motioned at his very full plate.

"Dennis was very generous," Gregory said, smiling.

"Dennis runs a tight ship. And he's been here since forever and thoroughly enjoys his work and the people."

"It shows," Gregory admitted. "It's nice to see someone who truly enjoys his work."

"Well, the potatoes are real," she said, laughing, "and the desserts are really made from scratch, so, whenever you're done with round one, feel free to go get round two." She winked at Meredith and left.

Chapter 4

MEREDITH APPRECIATED THE break in the conversation. She wasn't ready to get into their history, and she was in no way ready to get into their future. She motioned at his plate. "Are you likely to eat more?"

"I don't know," he said. "Hard to say. ... I've got rather a lot here. But that's not the same thing as dessert."

"Right, dessert is a back-tummy thing."

He chuckled. "Absolutely. Besides, you know I've always had a sweet tooth."

At that, she stopped and then shrugged. "Well, the person I knew a few years ago is different from the person I'm with right now," she said. "Honestly, I don't remember that you had a sweet tooth." Immediately after she said that, the conversation froze again. When somebody called her name from the far side, she looked over to see Stan walking toward her.

"Here comes the vet," she said, "so, if you want to ask any questions about downstairs, this is your opportunity." She looked at Gregory to see the frustration on his face. Good, that's how she felt inside too. She didn't know if he felt that way because they were always being interrupted or because they weren't ready to have a conversation on their history. She didn't really know that she wanted to have that conversation either.

Everything about his reappearance in her life was just so much out of the blue that she found it confusing. He had arrived in her world years ago and had taken up every moment of her time, and then she'd ended up losing him almost as fast. Now she was stuck wondering if she even wanted to open any doors again.

But she needed to be friendly. Professionally speaking. For his sake and her own. It was also very important for his healing, and, although she had a hard time with his decision back then, she was as much to blame as he was, and she supposed they did need to clear the air. Otherwise, it would be hard for both of them to move on.

But it was all happening so fast that she wasn't having any chance to reassess or to consider the implications of his presence now.

He was a good person, ... a really good person, but, if he wasn't for her, she would be fine with that. At least she had been fine all these years in his absence. Professionally, she wanted to make sure he got back on his feet, but personally, she wanted to see him move forward as a happy, healthy, well-adjusted male, entering a new stage of his life.

Then maybe she could too.

She wanted to think that she had nothing to still deal with in regard to their relationship, but she knew that there was. As it stood, she was determined to be as much of a pro as she could possibly be, to do what she needed to do to help him heal and to stay friendly but to not get involved.

Now, if only she could trust her heart to follow through with her plan.

"What's with the serious thoughts?" Stan asked as he arrived, a big smile on his face.

She looked up at him, gave him a half a smile and said,

"Stan, meet Gregory. He's a new arrival."

Gregory reached up to shake his hand only to see that he had something small and rust-colored in his arms. "And who is that?" he asked in delight.

Stan chuckled. "This is Morgan. He's got some long ridiculous pedigree name." Stan smiled. "But this little guy has abandonment issues right now. His mom was supposed to be here to pick him up a couple hours ago, and she got a flat tire and is delayed, so, if he's in his cage, he hollers and whines and breaks my heart. Therefore, I'm wandering around, introducing him to everybody."

Immediately Gregory reached out to pet the little rust-colored Maltese. "He's adorable."

"And not really appropriate to bring around food, what with all his long hair," Stan said. "I came to grab a coffee, and I was going to take him outside for a bit, but then I saw lovely Meredith here, and I know how much she loves puppies."

"I don't think there's anything that wears fur that I don't love," Meredith confessed, pushing her empty plate back and adjusting her chair slightly. "May I hold him?"

Stan gently passed the little dog over, who immediately licked Meredith's neck and chin. She chuckled. "He's lovely."

"If you can hang on to him for a sec, I'll grab a coffee." And, just like that, Stan disappeared.

She laughed and scratched the little guy as he woofed slightly and snuggled in closer. She looked over at Gregory, a big grin on her face. "See? There are huge advantages to being here," she said.

"For patients *and* staff apparently," he said. "I half want to cuddle him myself, but I'm still eating."

"And that's the disadvantage of taking so much food," Meredith teased. "I was done in half the time."

"You just ate too fast," he said. "I, on the other hand, am enjoying my meal."

"That's one way to look at it." She snickered. "I often visit the clinic, spending some time with the foster animals. They all need love."

"It's great that this option is here," Gregory said. "For the patients, it's got to be a huge factor in their healing."

"A lot of the animals need rehabilitation too because they're petrified of people or are a little aggressive," she said. "We integrate them slowly with our human patients, giving these abused animals time to get to know each other and then to get adjusted to being around the people here." She kept on snuggling the dog while she spoke. "Most of our human patients are a whole lot slower at dealing with the animals, so the animals already sense that they're injured and that they're not as dangerous as some two-legged people." She spoke softly, her tone holding no judgment or pity. "And, like this little guy here, he's just lonely and wants to be loved."

"I think that describes the ongoing state for a lot of us," Gregory said in a cryptic remark.

She wondered at it but kept her voice low as she replied simply, "True enough." Meredith avoided his gaze the entire time, instead focusing on wrapping both arms around the puppy and hugging him affectionately. Seeing Stan coming toward her, Meredith stood. "Can you carry him and your coffee, or do you want me to come with you?"

He laughed in delight. "You just want to come and spend time with this little guy."

"That's true." She didn't deny it. Glancing down at

Gregory, Meredith bade him goodbye as she picked up her tray with her free hand, then filled it with her empty dishes and disappeared.

Sure, it was running away. But sometimes taking the closest exit was the smartest thing. Gregory would be here for months, and there would be an awful lot of stress and tough times ahead for him. And for her. They had time to talk. And she wouldn't push it right now.

She smiled at Stan as they took the back door down one level.

Stan looked at her and said, "Something in that exit of yours looked like you were escaping."

"Absolutely," she said. "We had a thing five years ago. I didn't want him to go back into the navy, and he went."

"Ouch," he said. "Yeah, definitely going to be some fun times ahead."

"No," she responded. "Not really. He made a new life for himself, and I've made a new life for myself too."

"I don't believe that. From just those thirty seconds I spent around you two, I can feel the pent-up emotions. You've both got something to say to the other one. Maybe you and Gregory have been putting in the time to make it through the last five years, but circumstances have thrown you back together again," he said with a gentle smile. "There's a reason for that."

"Sure," she said. "It's called closure."

WELL, GREGORY GOT to spend some time with her. Obviously a lot of the people here were her friends, maybe even her family, in a loose way for her.

It had been nice to have her company over dinner. Yet she wouldn't stick around just because of him. Maybe if things had gone differently five years ago, but they hadn't. So, once again, he was the odd man out. A state Gregory should be used to but wasn't.

Ever since he'd walked away from her, he'd found it difficult to adjust. His buddies had joked and had bugged him about it, and he had definitely been a good friend and a well-respected and revered part of their SEALs team, but he had felt differently after he and Meredith broke up. As if he'd left a part of himself behind. A part of himself that he knew he could never reclaim because of their circumstances. Because of their professional passions. Which unfortunately had been at odds with their personal passions.

Now here he was with her, and it was just a little too stunning to believe. He'd been shocked when he'd been accepted, then overjoyed, followed by complete panic. On the other hand, the food at this one-of-a-kind rehab center was delicious, and that filled a gaping appetite within him. Looking at Meredith revived another kind of appetite. But she was out of bounds to him now. By the time he finished eating and pushed his plate back, he was stuffed.

Dennis walked over with a big smirk on his face. "Well?"

"Delicious," Gregory stated. "I was looking forward to trying out your desserts, but I'm too full."

"You can take something back to your room," Dennis said. "The one thing we do ask is that you not waste food. You're welcome to all you can eat, but, if you're not going to eat it, don't take it."

"That makes sense," he said. "Keeps costs down too."

"It's the only way to keep costs down and to keep the quality of the food up. So it's all good. You're welcome to anything and everything you want, just make sure that you try to eat it."

"I've got no problem with that," Gregory said. "I'm going to make my way over there and grab a cup of coffee."

"No need," he said. "I'll grab you one. Do you want cream or sugar?"

"Black," Gregory said with a smirk. "Always pure black and strong."

"I'll see what I can do."

Gregory watched as Dennis walked over, disposed of the tray of dishes on a big shelf that slipped through to the kitchen side and then poured a cup of coffee. As he returned, he said, "I've got fresh cinnamon buns coming out of the oven. They're actually out now. We just iced them. … Do you want one?"

It was beyond him to say no, so he nodded and said, "I'll sit here outside and try to recover from my trip, while I wait for room to show up in my stomach to eat that dessert. I presume tomorrow will start with a bang for me, and I guess this might be the last night I'll enjoy myself for a while." Gregory said it with a laugh, but he knew that some rehab sessions were brutally painful.

Dennis nodded. "I'm glad to see you know what's coming," he said. "It's always so sad when I see somebody new, and they have no clue what to expect. I don't know where they get the idea that a pill will fix them or an hour in a hot tub, like this is some spa or retreat. I guess it's our general drive-through mentality coupled with our dependence on convenience. But that first day of PT will knock any misconceptions right out of them. It usually takes about six weeks before I see them again looking anything but agonized."

"Are the therapists good here?" Gregory hated the note of anxiety in his voice and the nagging little voice in his head that slammed him for being more focused on Meredith than on the level of care Gregory might find here. Not that he hadn't checked out some credentials here. But he would admit his main focus had been elsewhere. Besides, as far as his previous rehab center had been concerned, Gregory didn't need to come here at all. But he had disagreed because he certainly wasn't back to fit form, even for his new reality, and what Gregory wanted was to be as strong and as capable as he could be. In the present, given these new circumstances for him.

"They're very good," Dennis said, turning around to face him. "They'll get you into shape, but you may not like their methods."

"I've been beaten up by a lot of therapists before," he replied with a crooked grin. "I'm hoping for a helping hand that will unlock the secrets to getting my strength back. I have so many injuries that my body is still in shock."

Dennis pondered that for a while before speaking. "Then you need to cut back on the meat and triple your vegetable intake to load up your body with the most nutrients possible from a variety of colorful foods that are easily digestible, saving your body's energy for the more important healing matters," he suggested. "Also the carbs can be eased back into your body slowly. After all, your body has enough healing to deal with right now. It needs its energy to be directed to that healing. Yes, these carbs are good for almost instant energy, but, if you flood your system with too much insulin, it'll make you tired, and your body won't give you the best performance of your life."

At that, Gregory laughed. "Well, I certainly agree with

some of that. I'm guessing you have a dietitian on staff, right?"

Dennis nodded. "I think we've got every medical-related profession covered in here. As soon as you think there's a problem in any one direction, make sure you talk to somebody. Somebody here can give you a hand. Be right back." Dennis returned a few moments later with a huge cinnamon bun slathered in cream cheese icing. Handing him a fork, he spoke, "It's still pretty hot. You might want to use that." He disappeared into the crowd again.

Gregory looked around to see the groups at the various tables had shifted and reformed with new groups, new people and new conversations. Several were out on the deck with him as the sun was still high. It was hot out here, but he didn't want to go inside yet. He had felt smothered in the hospital environment. And not much less so in his previous rehab location. He still craved fresh air. But he also felt the fatigue, probably from the large dinner as Dennis had mentioned.

Not to mention the excitement and the stress of traveling and knowing he would meet Meredith again. And then, of course, meeting her, actually having dinner with her, and yet, searching for that same connection that they'd shared before, and not finding it had been draining. He could handle the physical stressors much easier than the emotional ones.

He didn't know if their connection was gone because too much time had passed or because she had deliberately detached from him. He wouldn't blame her if she had.

He'd had such high hopes when he'd realized he was coming here, and, right now, it looked like all of them were dashed.

Chapter 5

MEREDITH DIDN'T TRY to avoid Gregory for the next few days, but she did not go out of her way to stop in and say hi either. She did her job and carried on.

As it was, the staffing was a little challenging as one of the nurses went down sick, and another one was off on holiday, so routines got shuffled around, and job duties got shuffled around with them. On Gregory's third day here, she ended up going to his room, back on his schedule as his day nurse. As she walked into his room, he looked up and smiled in surprise.

"Hey, I haven't seen you in a while. Figured maybe you were avoiding me."

"Of course not," she said with a frown. "I've got no reason to. It's just been crazy busy."

He nodded, but it was a small nod. His gaze seemed searching.

She smiled reassuringly at him. "One of the nurses is on holiday, and one's sick, so we all have to pitch in to cover these absences. We don't have enough staff as it is, but Dani is interviewing. It takes time to find qualified people," she explained. Then wondered if giving that many details made her seem defensive. She mentally shook her head. *You're his primary care nurse.*

He settled back ever-so-slightly.

"How are you settling in?" she asked.

"Good," he said. "It's been pretty easy so far. ... Almost like a holiday here." He had a big grin on his face.

She smirked. "Well, it is, until it isn't."

He grimaced at that. "I hear you, but, so far, there's been nothing I haven't handled easily."

"But you're still in the testing stage, aren't you?"

"Yes," he said, "it seems like it. Every day they run me through another gamut of tests, whether its blood work, lab work, physio work, mental work, emotional work or something else." He shook his head in disgust.

She laughed at that. "Well, what we ultimately want, when you get out of here, is a whole, healthy, strong person, and, if you're lacking development in any of those areas," she said, "then you're in trouble all around."

"I get the theory of that, but waiting to get started isn't much fun."

"Gotcha." She finished checking him over. "Maybe this afternoon you will begin the real work."

"I hope so. I'm starting to feel a little guilty even being here and taking up a bed as I'm not as bad as the rest of these guys."

"You mean, the ones who wince and groan as they get up and get a cup of coffee and head back at a turtle's pace and walk like they're old men?" she asked, withholding her grin.

"Exactly, then I find out some of them have been here for a long time, and I realize how good I'm actually doing."

"Well, I wouldn't worry about it," she said. "Once you start your PT, you might find you're a little more related to those older-looking men than you think."

He shook his head. "Not likely. I've already done lots of

months of rehab."

She didn't say anything at that, just smiled gently. "Let's hope in a couple days you feel the same way."

Meredith knew that Gregory was following the pattern of a lot of the young men who came into this rehab center; coming in strong, a little bit arrogant and some of them cocky, they thought they could handle whatever was thrown at them. Once the staff started them on their custom programs, they broke down very quickly. She didn't want to see Gregory at that stage, but she also knew how important it was for the therapists to get rid of that ego and to start digging in deep and finding out who the patients were and what they really wanted in their life and from their bodies.

Everyone needed to find out whether Gregory was prepared to work for the intended results or not.

Physiotherapy wasn't for sissies, and, when they had multiple injuries—like Gregory, who'd come to a certain point and hadn't progressed further—then it was time for a change, and, in this case, it would be a big disruptive change because nobody here did things quite the same way as they did at other rehab places.

She'd heard it time and time again. It started as a holiday but then almost turned into a prison camp by the time they got started because the rehab work required was intense and a lot was demanded of the patients. Now the good news was that, on the other end all that hard work, it paid off in spades, and the patients were overjoyed to be who they became.

The journey was not easy—or fast—nor was it something that they could take lightly. A lot of soul-searching went on. A lot of getting to the bottom of what was holding them back. They did have a psychologist on staff, and every patient had sessions with him. It was very important to make sure that the mental and emotional state of these patients was as healthy as their physical state, and, most of the time, these internal states were often in worse shape.

Some of these men had PTSD, and some had survived incredible traumas and losses: friends dying in front of them, commanders walking away, and sometimes whole teams being blown up, their lives with them.

She hadn't attended any of those sessions because, of course, they were personal and private for the patients, but she'd heard from some of the men afterward about just how eye-opening those sessions were. But only after the men had reached a turning point, where they would actually discuss what they'd been through. And some of the men took months and months and months to get to that point. Some of them were much more open, in touch with who they were before they got here.

But she didn't think Gregory would fit that category. But then, she could be wrong. It had been five years. Five very long years, and she, for one, had changed a lot. But now that she looked at him, she wondered if the changes she had gone through were all that good or if she'd changed all that much. She hadn't been stressed physically as much as he had; she hadn't been as challenged emotionally as he had; she hadn't even had to walk away from her career as he had. And, in many ways, she wondered if she'd changed at all.

GREGORY WATCHED HER leave with a thoughtful expression on his face. He had worried that she was avoiding him. That wasn't what he wanted between them; to at least be friends would be nice. But, he had to admit, to be more than that would be better.

A hard knock came on the door, and he looked up to see Shane—his assigned therapist. He came into Gregory's room, rubbing his hands together, gleefully saying, "You ready?"

Gregory nodded. "I am."

"Well, you'll know for sure pretty soon," Shane said. He was a huge, six foot four, strappingly muscled man, but it was lean muscle, and he always carried a bright cheerfulness that Gregory envied.

Shane motioned at the wheelchair and said, "Come on in that. We'll head over to the first room."

"Why the wheelchair?" Gregory asked. He'd been to a lot of different therapy sessions, and he highly doubted it would be anything much. He'd done very well before, and his former therapists had always been positive and cheerful, giving Gregory lots of praise. He didn't see how it would be any different here. Matter of fact, he was back to feeling guilty that he was even wasting their time.

Shane looked at him and said, "Trust me. The wheelchair might look easy now, but you'll want it when you come back."

Frowning at that and hoping Shane was wrong, Gregory made his way to the wheelchair, sat down and slowly wheeled his way behind Shane.

Shane walked in a steady line to one of the rooms Gregory had been in earlier for some testing. Shane motioned to him. "Wheel over to the side and stand up, then hop over here to this mat," he said.

"What are we starting with?" Gregory asked as he followed the instructions.

Once he sat on the mat, Shane said, "We'll start with floor work, and I'm telling you right now, anytime that we get to a point where you need to stop, you must say so. There's no shame in telling me to stop. I'm the only one who will hear you say it. When we hit a pain level of six out of ten, I want to hear about it. You'll do your body more harm than good if you overstress it."

Gregory just waved his hand at him. "I'll be fine. What do you want me to do?"

Shane sighed gently, as if he had seen and heard that many, many times, but then he launched into a three-hour session that started off easy. But, by the time he was done, Gregory lay on the mat on his back, his body completely filmed in sweat, visible tremors racking up and down his spine.

He didn't know what had just happened, but it was something completely different than what he had expected. And he realized just how useless all his previous therapy sessions had been.

Maybe his previous therapists had given him too much positive reinforcement and hadn't bothered to make him work. But no way would Shane let Gregory off the hook on anything. Shane wanted results, and, according to him, he would get them. It made things very difficult for Gregory when he lay here in shock on the floor, wanting to cry like a baby.

Shane squatted beside him. "How are you doing?"

"I'm fine," he gasped out.

"Well, you're not fine," Shane said. "And you didn't tell me to stop either."

Gregory winced at that.

Shane saw that and nodded. "You can't let your pride or

your ego come between you and a therapy session," he said. "That's never a good thing."

"How would I know?" he asked.

"Know what? That I would put you through the paces? Well, if you must know, I took it easy on you today," he said. "I was watching to see at what point you would say something and realized you just wouldn't. Because, for you, it's still all about saving face and still all about being the best, and it's still all about giving a presentation instead of actually being true and honest to the broken body that you're currently living with. And you have to get rid of all that.

"If you want to get back to where you were, if you want to be that strong, capable, vibrant man that you see yourself as in your head, then you must let go of all that facade. Now you've got about forty-five minutes until dinnertime. I suggest you head back to your room and get a shower, and we'll start again tomorrow." He got up, seemingly unconcerned, and walked over to make some notes on his tablet.

Gregory lay on the floor, his body so damn weak that he doubted he could make it to his wheelchair, but he'd be damned if he'd ask for help. He rolled over, got up and swayed.

Instantly Shane was there, gripping his forearm. "Remember that thing about pride?" he scolded.

And Gregory, for once, almost felt shame. "Now that you're here," he gasped, "can you get me to my wheelchair?"

"The easiest way is to bring the wheelchair to you," Shane replied. He shifted his position, reached out, snagged it, twirled it around and brought it up right behind Gregory so he could sit down.

Once he'd collapsed, Gregory slowly turned his wheelchair toward the door without saying another word to Shane and headed out.

With all his training, Gregory had always expected to be the best, and somehow he thought he was still. Somehow he thought he had been giving his all and doing everything exactly as he needed to.

Yet always a little bit of him wondered if he had been fooling himself, but he had ignored that nudging.

Slowly, moving as carefully as he could, he made his way to his room, and, as soon as he had the door closed, he leaned back, closed his eyes and cried.

Chapter 6

MEREDITH CAME AROUND the corner to see Gregory on his way to his bedroom ... and caught sight of his face. He'd found out the reality of being here. She knew Gregory had Shane on his team. Shane was many, many things, and some would say he was a taskmaster, but he was also a good guy, and he wouldn't push Gregory farther than he had to go, but Shane would push Gregory right up to that level. And obviously, Gregory's introduction was a little more than he'd expected.

She walked a few steps, wondering if she should knock on his door—when she heard him sob. Immediately her hand went to her mouth, and her heart broke. She hustled away before anybody else realized what was going on and then ran to sit in the privacy of her on-site living quarters, wondering what she should do.

Her shift had ended an hour ago. She had planned to go for an early dinner, but realizing he was as hurt as he was, ... should she check in on him? Would he even answer her? Would he answer anybody today?

Obviously today had been hard—physically and mentally and emotionally—and, if he knew he wasn't alone, maybe it would help. Then again, right now he probably only wanted to be alone. Still warring with herself, she quickly changed, checked the time and realized he'd had a good half hour to shower and potentially pull himself together again. Maybe she'd go by his room again and just knock.

Walking past his room, she stopped, hesitated, then rapped hard. There was no answer. She frowned because she'd seen him go inside. It was possible he'd already headed to dinner; the only other option was he was possibly asleep. She knocked again and thought she heard something on the other side.

"Gregory, it's Meredith." She waited and then said in a more authoritative voice, "Let me in."

"The door is unlocked," he said, bristling.

She reached for the handle to check, and it was, indeed, unlocked. She opened the door. The patient's room doors all had locks, but the medical staff had keys if they needed to open any. It was a patient's right to have privacy, but it wasn't right to lock everybody out, not in a medical facility like this one.

She stepped inside and took one look at him. He sat on his bed, just a towel around his waist, his body stiff, as if putting on a casual, *Hey, I'm fine, good enough* show. Meredith may have been fooled if she hadn't heard him crying earlier.

"I was wondering if you felt up for dinner." She saw the whisper of pain across his face. "I know you had your first session today with Shane. He's a really good guy," she said, knowing she was rambling on but unable to stop herself. "And he's fair, but he's also tough. I know he would have worked you hard today. So, if you want to crash on your bed, maybe I can bring you something." He looked at her, and she could see him warring with the idea. "Remember. It's not a weakness to accept help," she said gently. She watched as his shoulders sagged, and then his chest deflated.

"Honestly," he finally spoke, "I'm not sure I could make it out there."

Meredith nodded briskly, her compassionate understanding written all over her face. "What would you like for dinner?"

"I'm not … I'm not even hungry."

"And that's one of the reasons I wanted to check on you. To get you some food. You need to keep fueling that body. You need good healthy food, and you need to keep those nutrients flowing to heal properly," she said.

"In that case, just bring me whatever you think I need." He waved a hand at her. "I'm so damn tired, I don't think I can even get pants on."

Meredith walked over to his chest of drawers and pulled open the top one. "How about a pair of boxers or just a pair of sleep pants?" She held them both up as she walked over to him. He frowned at them and chose the boxers.

She gave him the boxers, folded the others and laid them on the small table. "If you want to put these pants on, then fine, you can do that too," she said. "If they're still here when I come back, I'll put them back in the drawer." With that, Meredith turned and headed to the door.

"Meredith …"

She spun and looked at him, raising an eyebrow. "Yes, Gregory. What's up?"

He hesitated, and she could see how hard this was for him. Finally, he managed to say, "Thanks."

She beamed at him and quickly left his room. It was either that or cry. To see a strong man come to the point of crying was very heartbreaking, but it was also heartwarming. He had a long way to go, but it sounded like he was on his way. And that was worth so much.

She didn't know who he was right now, but she liked the man she saw. Maybe even more than the Gregory she'd met five years ago. This one had something about him that just endeared him to her. It wasn't like she collected lame ducks or broken bits of humanity, but to see the strength and to see that humanity inside Gregory now come out in full force? ... Well, it was worth everything to her.

KNOWING HIS ENERGY was quickly fading, Gregory managed to get the boxers on and laid the towel over the small table. Standing up just long enough to pull down the bedcovers, he collapsed on the bed, already tilted upward. That way he could rest—or eat—in a seated position, and he closed his eyes.

Meredith's offer had come at a perfect time. Gregory was grateful he didn't have to go to the cafeteria for dinner. He was also a little worried about her seeing him like this, but it was obvious that she had seen how he felt regardless, so his act of looking strong and not in crappy shape hadn't worked. He hadn't really expected to have a real hope for a relationship with her, but there was always a chance. Still ... it wasn't looking so good to date.

He reached for the sleep pants, struggled to get them on, and then, panting, he collapsed back on the bed. He knew it would take time for his heart rate to calm down and for his sense of complete exhaustion to disappear.

It was early, ... only like five-thirty p.m., but hopefully, with any luck, he'd feel better after dinner. Right now he knew he wasn't leaving his bed for the rest of the evening. He'd been warned, but he'd just been so sure that he knew what to expect …

Something that gave him both hope and trepidation was the thought that tomorrow was another day, and he would face Shane again. Now the good news was that he knew—if he could keep up with Shane's onslaught of physical rehab— that, in six weeks, Gregory would be incredibly improved. Getting to that point though … was tenuous at best.

Gregory had never turned his back on a challenge before.

He just hadn't thought he would face this kind of challenge. He'd thought this would be minor.

Maybe it had been his way of dealing with the fact that so little was going on in his world that he thought this would be nothing, when, in truth, this was incredible. He dozed off, and then woke up when he heard someone call him. He opened his eyes to see Meredith handing something to him.

"You ready for food?"

"Sure," he murmured, shifting. "Sorry. I'm exhausted."

"I know," she said. "I can hear it in your voice. Do you want help to sit up?"

He shook his head. "I'm trying to figure out how these beds work."

"This is one of the new ones, so everything is adjustable." She quickly showed him the remote and how it worked. With a couple adjustments, he sat almost upright. She brought the small table closer to the side of the bed and placed his tray on it.

As he looked around, she had also brought in a small trolley, and a ton of food was there. "Are you eating too?"

She hesitated and then asked, "Is that okay?"

"Of course," he said. "I'm delighted to have the company."

"I didn't want you to eat alone," she said. "But if you'd

prefer to or to eat later, that's fine."

"Please," he said, "join me." He turned to look at the tray in front of him. "Wow, how did you know that I absolutely love meat pies?"

"I didn't know, but it is one of Dennis's favorite dishes, and he does an incredible job on these. So, when I saw them, I figured you might like one."

"They're homemade?"

"Well, if you're asking if Dennis made them, yes, he did."

Gregory bent to cut into the crust and watched as the steam rose from the center. "You're really lucky to have him."

"Absolutely," Meredith said. "But, at the same time, I think he loves being here. So, if anything, it's a mutual admiration."

He chuckled at that. "There's a lot worse things in life." The trolley was in front of her, like a table. "Can you eat like that?" he asked.

"I was going to put the tray on my lap," she said as she moved her tray off the trolley and sat down on the visitor's chair with her legs lifted on the balls of her feet.

"As long as you're comfortable," he said.

"I've never been better. Now eat."

"I notice an awful lot of green on my plate," he groaned, studying the food choices.

"Yes, you need the vegetables."

"It'll take weeks of inhaling vegetables to notice a difference in my body."

"Were you planning on doing anything in those weeks other than to be here and to try to heal?"

He stopped, frowned, looked at her and said, "Okay,

that was mean."

She laughed. "Not really. If you don't give your body what it needs, it has to take it from your stores. And you don't have any stores to give it, so buck up, and start eating properly."

"But I like my potatoes," he complained.

"And you have a couple," she said, "but you have a lot more veggies. And, when you're done with all those veggies, I brought you a salad."

He stared at her in horror.

She laughed out loud. "But you like salad."

"But I'd rather have the meat pies," he said.

"We're back to the fact that you told me to get whatever you need, so I did."

He looked at her plate and said, "You have mostly green."

"I love vegetables," she said with a smile. "I know how important they are for me too."

"And what if I don't quite like vegetables so much?" He stabbed a fork into the broccoli and picked up a piece, studied it for a long moment, then popped it into his mouth. He lifted his eyebrows. "Okay, so this broccoli is really good."

"All broccoli is really good," she corrected.

He shook his head but found himself craving the vegetables, and, before long, they were all gone. He stared at his empty plate in amazement. "Dennis has a swift hand with vegetables too," he said.

"Absolutely," she said. "And, if you eat the salad and everything else, you get dessert."

"What if, instead of dessert, I want another meat pie?" he asked craftily.

"If you think you can still eat it, then you can have it." She laughed. "I'll cheerfully go down and get it for you. We just ask that, whatever you take, you eat."

"And that's a good rule. I wish the entire world would follow it. I've seen too many starving children the world over, and yet, back here, we're so overfed that we're dumping food on a daily basis. It's criminal!"

"Not until they change the laws, it isn't." She sighed. "But it's one of the things that we're strict about here. In order to keep the food quality up, we have to keep the costs down, and that means less waste." She laughed suddenly. "Now I sound like Dennis."

"Well, those meat pies are never going to waste." But suddenly Gregory came to the bottom of his salad bowl and realized he was really stuffed. "I don't think I can even eat another meat pie, and that just breaks my heart."

"If you want, I can ask him to save you one for lunch tomorrow."

He turned and looked at her in surprise. "Would he do that?" he asked hopefully.

She laughed. "He has no problem doing that."

"If there are any left …"

She nodded. "When I go get us coffee, I'll ask him. Doesn't mean there are many left, but, if there are, I'm sure he'd be happy to put away a couple for you."

Gregory smiled. "And I would love that. Thank you."

He watched as she ate at a much slower pace than him. She still had a whole bowl of salad to get through. But she worked away, quite happily enjoying every bite. That had been one of the things he'd always remembered about her. She'd lived life to the fullest, enjoying everything. Whether it was a glass of water, the sunshine, or the sound of a bird, it had always amazed him. He'd been much more of a go-getter type, while she had been happy to sit and relax.

Gregory had never really found a way to relax back then, but, ever since his hospitalization, he'd had more than enough time to sit still and to think about life. He hadn't yet found the art of enjoying stillness, but even here—having her eat her meal like she was—it's like she didn't want to be anywhere else. And he couldn't be happier with that thought.

Chapter 7

MEREDITH WOKE UP the next morning feeling a little sick. Maybe she was just tired; maybe she caught the flu that was going around. Or maybe it was the excitement of finally having Gregory here. So much worrying, so much waiting, and now he was here. She had a flashback of his first couple days, and they had survived. Some sort of camaraderie existed between them. Not exactly a friendship—she felt more professional toward him than anything—but, on the inside, she still had that little bit of anxiety. She wasn't sure what that meant.

He'd looked so beaten and so sore last night that she couldn't help but be nice. But she in no way flattered herself to think that they had a friendship. A lot of relationships came and went here, along with the patients; however, she knew of at least a half-dozen relationships that had stuck solid.

But that didn't mean that anything was here between her and Gregory at this point. In fact, as she got up and had her shower, she couldn't think of anything that was between them at all. Still, she quickly dressed and headed out for breakfast and then to work.

As she walked into her office, she found stacks of folders waiting for her. She looked at an update note and realized several patients had had bad nights, and the night nurse had been backed up. As Meredith read through the names, she winced to see Gregory's name there as well.

She checked through to see who she would have to spend a little bit more time watching over, and only three of those who'd had night disturbances made that list. She wasn't alone on day shift either, which was a good thing. As she glanced at the stack of papers beside her, she groaned. They kept both paper files and digital files, and everything had to correlate and be updated. It was the only way to be assured that things were accurate. And some things, like scans, just didn't have the same visual on an iPad as they did when up on the backlit screens. She grabbed her list and started her rounds. She left Gregory for last, and, as she walked in, she found him still sleeping.

She frowned, realizing how much of a bad night he'd had to still be sleeping at nine-thirty a.m. She stepped out into the hallway and sent a note to his team, letting them know his bad night had resulted in a late morning, and he still wasn't moving.

Back in her office, she worked on the stack of files because now she also had her own to update. By the time she looked up again, it was already eleven a.m. She quickly grabbed her tablet and headed to check on Gregory again. As she knocked on the door and heard his muffled voice, she stepped in, looked at him and smiled. "Hey, sleepyhead."

He lifted blurry eyes and stared at her. "What time is it?"

"It's eleven am."

Gregory stared at her in shock; then, groaning loudly, he rolled over but didn't get out of bed.

"I hear you had a bad night," she said, using her most professional voice. She walked over and quickly took his temperature and blood pressure. His blood pressure was definitely up, but his temperature was fine. She looked at him and asked, "Have you been up yet?"

He shook his head. "No, not yet. Not looking forward to it either."

"Do you want me to stay here in case you have trouble?" He shot her a look. She smiled but stood firm. "You have to tell me to leave, if that's what that look was supposed to be."

"Yes," he said, "you can leave."

She frowned. "When you're a little more awake, take a look at what you missed this morning. Also potentially head for an early lunch so that you're a little more prepared for the PT this afternoon."

"I don't think I'm going to physio this afternoon," he said. He got up, grabbed one crutch and walked past her slowly, like an old man, bent over slightly. His gait was getting better as he made it to the bathroom. He was still hobbling but looked a lot less like he was crippled by the time he made it there.

She stood and waited.

When he stepped out, he looked at her and frowned.

"Yes, I'm still here," she said. "This is still my job."

At that, he didn't say anything but glanced at the floor. He made his way back to the bed and sagged. "I'm not going anywhere today," he said.

"Not even for food?"

"Not at this moment," he said. "Maybe later. I think I'll go back to sleep." He stretched out, rolled over and dropped his head on the pillow, groaning with each move.

Yet she knew he was holding back. She walked back outside his room, closed the door behind her, made several more notations and then sent a note to Shane, Gregory's physiotherapist. By the time she was back to her office and working again, she looked up to see Shane standing there, his arms crossed over his chest. "Is he sleeping again?"

"I don't know. Probably," she said. "I know he was pretty worn out late yesterday into this morning."

"I know," he said, taking a seat in her office. "I was still testing him yesterday, but I did put him through quite a few paces. I also watched to see when it was too much."

"I have a note here from Anna, who was on overnight, and apparently it was a lot too much. She says he woke up with pretty rough cramps and lots of abdominal pain." Meredith handed him the notes.

Shane looked them over, mentally ticked them off, nodded and said, "I'll take a look at him now." He got up.

As he walked from her office, she called out, "Don't forget. We might need to bring in one of his doctors on this too."

"I'm on it," Shane replied from the distance.

She could hear his footsteps disappearing. She worried about Gregory for a few moments and then realized that it wasn't her job. Not this part at least. He had a medical team, and they were a damn good team. They would take care of him in each of their specialized and distinctive practices, as she would take care of all her patients as their nurse. Another one from last night, who had had a bad time of it, she'd already visited twice, but he hadn't been doing so well either.

She grabbed her tablet and headed back to see him, sitting up in bed, looking a whole lot older than she'd ever seen him before. "Wow, Solson, you don't look too good," she said.

"Don't feel too good either," he replied. "I think I must have picked up the flu or something."

"Do you want me to bring you some food?" she asked.

He frowned, thought about it and then said, "No, I was thinking that maybe fresh air would help."

"And it might," she said encouragingly. "Do you want me to help you out on the cafeteria deck? Maybe snag a coffee on the way past?"

He looked at her, pathetically grateful. "If you wouldn't mind, that would help a lot."

She helped him into the wheelchair.

Solson nodded. "I was hoping there might be a shady spot where I can get some fresh air, maybe sitting closer to the doors on the deck? Have a juice or something for my stomach?"

"Well, let's go take a look," she said. "Did you have anything different last night? Any change in medication I don't know about?"

"No," he said, "it's such a weird thing. I had cramps, and my head just boomed, and my back started to hurt."

"Interesting," she said, "and it came on suddenly?"

"Yes, very," he said. "It didn't make a whole lot of sense. But I am feeling a bit better now that I am moving."

"Did you end up with vomiting or diarrhea?"

"Both," he said. "I wondered if it was maybe food poisoning." He stopped, frowned and said, "I did have some cookies last night."

"What kind of cookies?"

"They were butter cookies, but I've had them for a long time," he said. "I just woke up and got the munchies."

"Normally cookies dry out, but they don't cause that kind of an upset."

He gave her a sheepish look. "Well, I did eat the pack."

She stopped for a moment, walked around so she could look him in the face and asked, "You ate the whole pack of cookies? Was it full?"

He grinned and nodded. "I do have a sweet tooth."

"Well, that might make you have an upset stomach, with both vomiting and diarrhea," she said. "I'm scared to ask how many cookies there were."

He shrugged and mumbled something.

She wasn't sure what she heard, so she bent lower and repeated her question.

"Two dozen," he said, "maybe, give or take a few."

She tried to hold back her laughter, but there was no way. With her hand clapped over her mouth, she leaned against the wall and laughed and laughed. By the time she was done, he was grinning like a crazy man too.

"You don't do that enough," he said. "You should."

She smiled, shook her head and said, "I haven't heard anything that funny in a while. I mean, I hate to say that karma is right there, ready to bite you in the butt, however ..."

He nodded. "That's what I figured. I'm not sure it's all out yet either."

"Well, if it came out both ends, obviously your stomach revolted. So chances are something very light for lunch is about all you'll put down there today."

"That's what I was thinking. I thought I'd start with a glass of milk."

She grinned at that thought. "You do that." She led him gently through the cafeteria that wasn't busy yet and found him a spot outside where he was mostly in the shade, but he could shift if he needed to. "How does this look?"

"It looks good," he said. "I'll just sit here for a bit."

"Good, and I'll go get your milk," she said. Not giving him a chance to argue, she walked over to the large cooler and pulled out a carton of milk and brought it back for him. "Here you go," she said. "Now remember. Just take it easy at lunchtime. I know you always have a big appetite, but your stomach's really had a number done on it this time."

"Yeah," he said. "I guess I'm not a kid anymore."

"When you cross the thirty mark," she said, "your stomach isn't a kid anymore."

He chuckled, grinned and said, "Thanks, Meredith."

She patted his shoulder gently. "I'll check on you later." She walked back toward her office as a few more people came into the cafeteria. She took a side route and quickly walked down the line to see what there was for lunch. Apparently it was Mexican today. She smiled as she looked at the tacos, burritos, tortillas and guacamole, then said, "Dennis, this looks divine."

"Well, if it's so divine," he called out from the other side of the counter, where he was still loading up the sour cream and chives, "why are you going in the wrong direction?"

She grinned. "Because it's not time for my lunch yet," she said. "I'll be back in a little bit."

When she returned to her office, she quickly updated Solson's file. Most of the time he did well. But obviously a couple dozen butter cookies weren't what his stomach wanted last night. With those notes updated, she looked up to see one of the other nurses coming in. Rene plunked herself down and looked at Meredith, blew a wisp of hair off her forehead and said, "Wow, it's busy today."

"Apparently it's been busy for a while," she said, motioning at the stack of folders. "These here on the right side are still left over from the night shift." She pointed them out. "The rest are ours from today."

"I hear you," Rene said. "Most of the notes we can update as we go, but, when it comes to some of the other staff, we have to do the paperwork."

"There's always paperwork," Meredith said calmly. "Checks and balances. It's always about checks and balances."

"Right." Rene dropped her tablet on the table beside her and said, "I'll grab some food first, then get started on my own paperwork." She stopped, looking at Meredith, and asked, "Do you want to come?"

Meredith thought about it for a moment and then nodded. "Why not?" she said. "It's Mexican today too," she said to Rene.

"Wow," she said. "Let's go."

Laughing, the two women headed off.

GREGORY LAY ON his bed, exhausted. His muscles throbbed, and his body felt like he'd been tossed out into heavy uncharted seas and fought a twenty-mile swim against the tide before being smashed on the rocks and rescued just before he drowned. He'd already had a conversation with Shane, but Gregory wasn't at all sure that they were on the same wavelength. Gregory had overdone it and blamed himself, but he also blamed Shane for letting him.

"Well, it's an interesting reaction," Shane had said. "I was watching to make sure we didn't overdo things, but obviously something affected you."

"Yeah," Gregory said in a slightly bitter tone. "I can hardly even move today."

"And that also likely means a buildup of lactic acid in your system too," his therapist said thoughtfully. He walked over, sat down on the chair and appeared to be bringing up a file on his tablet. He clicked through several times and then shrugged. "Okay, well, I'll come back here after lunch. Then we'll do some exercises to loosen you up a little bit, making sure that you don't feel quite so bad, and see if we can get you back up on your feet again."

"Today?" Gregory asked in a rough, gravelly voice. He hated to be a whiner here, but none of this made any sense. If Shane had listened, why would they force him to do more? At the other place, as soon as Gregory was in pain, everything stopped until he healed.

"Well, a lot of the pain is from the muscles tightening up. As soon as you start moving again, the pain eases."

"Sure," he said. "What I can't handle is more pain. So whatever we do today, I'll need painkillers to even let you touch me."

"We can arrange for some of that," Shane said cheerfully. "What we can't do is let you just sit like this, where your muscles go cold and tight, creating a worse scenario tomorrow."

"Worse?" He damn-near glared at him. "One thing I can't do is get any worse."

"Exactly. So, do you want to work now so you can walk down to lunch—or at least wheel yourself down there on your own—or do you want us to bring you some food first? Only then you have to work with a full belly, and that won't be as easy."

"Not as easy?"

"It could be a little harder," Shane acknowledged. "There's just no right or wrong answer."

"Right," Gregory said, "so that sucks."

"Yes, it does. But those are the facts of life, ... so make a decision now." He stood here, hands on his hips, quietly waiting.

Gregory dropped back against his bed and said, "Now then. I don't think I could eat anyway."

"Exactly," he said. "Let's get those pajama bottoms off you, and we'll start on the ankles and the foot, working our way up."

"Sure, but that sounds completely backward," Gregory said. "It would make more sense to start at the thighs and work down."

His therapist smiled, while replying, "Well, we're working our way up first, and then we'll work our way down."

Gregory groaned. "Or you could just *not*."

"Well, it'll happen whether you like it or not," he said, his tone businesslike but determined, which pointed out to Gregory what a little whiny brat he was being.

He groaned. "Okay, let's do this."

And, for the next hour, Shane stretched, pulled, massaged and loosened up Gregory's muscles to the point that one leg and then his other shook out to not feeling too bad. By the time Shane had done Gregory's arms and chest and then was rolled over so Shane could work on his back, Gregory started to feel like a whole new man again.

"If I knew you could do this," Gregory said, "I would have called for you when I woke up."

"And that's exactly what you should have done," Shane replied. "Instead I heard it from Meredith."

"Yeah, she was here just after I woke up. I had to get up and go to the bathroom, and I guess I didn't look too good."

"Obviously," Shane chided. "That's just the way life is when you don't listen to your therapist."

"Right," Gregory replied. As he laid here, he realized his

body hummed with a sense of peace. "You have magical hands," he announced.

Shane laughed. "Years and years of experience. There's no need for pain here. Most of the time it's muscles that have been either not used for too long or we did too much. One of the other biggest issues is the fact that often you sleep too hard, too long and too deep, so the muscles don't even move around during the night. You sleep in one position. You wake up the next morning, and everything has seized up."

"Gotcha," he said. "Still sucks."

He laughed. "It does, indeed, but we're almost there." He stepped back a few moments later, looked down at Gregory and said, "Try to sit upright and see how you feel."

At that, Gregory rolled over, slowly sat up, rolled his shoulders and his neck, and said, "The shoulders are good. The arms are good. The neck is a bit tense."

Immediately Shane stepped behind him and quickly massaged the shoulder and neck joints. "How're your teeth? Do you grind your teeth at night?"

"I don't think so, but my jaw feels locked."

"That would explain the sore neck too." With those very experienced fingers, Shane gently but firmly massaged along the jawline and up along the TM joint under the ear and then moved up the outside of the ear, up across the temple and over the forehead before doing a quick down-the-head scalp rub.

By the time he was done, Gregory was almost ready to beg for more. "That last part of what you were doing," he said, "that's wickedly good."

Shane chuckled. "It is, isn't it?" he said. "Now get moving, and see how it is this time."

And, with that, Gregory slowly stood, hopped on one leg

along the length of the bed and then grabbed a crutch. He took a couple steps and turned around, calmly looking for his other crutch. He hobbled over, grabbed it and then did several steps around the room. "You know what? That feels pretty decent."

"Excellent. How about some lunch?"

Gregory nodded and said, "Yeah, that's probably good timing. I need to get changed though."

"Good. I'll see you down there. We'll do a session this afternoon," he said firmly. "It won't be hard, and we'll definitely do some lighter weights and multiple repetitions. Don't worry. We won't overwork it. I would suggest maybe an hour of that and then hit the pool."

At the sound of *pool*, Gregory lit up. "Now that would be ideal." He said, "Actually the hot tub too. That would really help to set this off."

"Maybe," Shane said. "But its food first, then some light workout, and afterward the pool before any hot tub time."

"Fine," he said in disgust. "Don't you ever give anybody a break?"

"No," Shane replied. "If we did that, everybody would want one." He laughed as he walked out.

Gregory pondered that, noting the laugh had left him feeling a hell of a lot better. He quickly got changed, and something about being dressed and ready to start the day seemed so different too. It felt good, like he had left the invalid part of him behind. He chose the wheelchair just because he didn't want to overdo it, and, as he rolled his way down the hallway and back to the cafeteria, he found most of the lunch crowd had come and gone. He rolled his way down the line, chose a selection of aromatic Mexican food and then headed to the sunshine, but, as soon as he got there, it was hot. Too hot. Struggling, he turned around, rolled back inside and found a table with a little more space for his wheelchair.

He hated the fact that he was still dealing with space issues while in wheelchairs, but it had been his choice, so it was what it was. He ate slowly, enjoying the food, but realizing, of course, he'd forgotten his water. It just seemed like everything was so much effort today. Even though Shane had done a heck of a job, everything appeared to be a lot more difficult. And maybe Gregory was just being forgetful from being so tired, but he looked over at the water several times and realized he couldn't avoid it. He rolled back and headed toward the drink section.

While he was there, he grabbed a bottle of water and then a cup of coffee. That made rolling his wheelchair a little harder, but he was determined to make it, and one wheel rotation at a time, he made his way to his table. Triumphant, he placed a full cup of coffee beside his plate and then opened the bottle of water. The trouble was, he drank it almost immediately.

Suddenly Dennis was there with a second bottle. "That was good work," he said in admiration. "I don't think I have ever seen anybody bring a cup of coffee over quite the same way."

Gregory shot him a look. "Right. I probably looked absolutely ridiculous."

"Nope, not at all," he said with a big grin. "It was good." He looked at Gregory's food and said, "How are you enjoying it?"

"I love it," he said, "but that's why I needed the water. It's a little spicy."

"We do like spicy food here."

"That's great," he said, "but some of it should come with a warning label."

Dennis smirked. "If this is too hot for you, I can get you something else."

"No, this will do just fine," he said, forking up another mouthful.

Dennis took off, leaving Gregory to finish his lunch in peace.

By the time he was done, he checked his watch and realized he was already late. Shane was likely waiting in the physio room for him already. But at least Gregory had dressed with that in mind. Moving slowly, he headed out to the hallway. There, he stopped and saw Meredith coming toward him. He frowned at her. "Are you looking for me?"

"Only to make sure that you're doing okay," she said gently.

And he hated that gentleness, that *Hey, I know you're injured, and I know you're hurt, and I just want to make sure you're fine* kind of thing because, like she'd said, it still was her job. And something about that struck him so wrong. It was just enough to piss him off.

He nodded stiffly and said, "I'm doing just fine, thanks. Shane was a good idea. Thank you for messaging him." And then, without another word, he turned the wheelchair in the direction he needed to go and rolled down the hallway, leaving her staring behind him.

He could feel her eyes burning into his back. When he reached this PT room, he tossed a quick glance back, and, sure enough, there she was, still staring at him.

Chapter 8

MEREDITH TRIED TO keep herself busy for the next few days and to not hover over Gregory. She didn't know whether it was the female part of her or the professional nurse part of her, but she figured it was likely a gentle mix of both. She also knew that that's the last thing Gregory wanted. He needed to move on with his life without feeling like somebody was affecting his progress. And that was fine with her. She had enough work to do. One of the other nurses had fallen sick, and Meredith was doing double duty right now. At the end of her day, she was tired and exhausted.

As Wednesday rolled around, she really needed to take some R&R just to feel better herself. As she quickly made her way through the day, she was busy without even minutes to spare until her shift was over. When she finally handed off her case files and clocked out for the day, she headed home to her on-site apartment, quickly changed into a bathing suit and headed back to the pool.

She was so tired that she didn't think she could do any laps but knew she needed to, just to destress. Nothing like physical exercise to wear some of that off, and she quickly dove in. She swam laps—one, two and three—and by the time she stopped at twenty, she realized she hadn't done as many as she needed to, but she already felt better. She did several more laps at a much slower pace. Instead of trying to plow through the water cleanly, she gently floated along the top and moved lightly.

A few more laps later, she took several deep breaths and floated to finish destressing. Finally, her body chilly, she headed over to the stairs. When she got out and wrapped herself with a towel, she noticed a few patients sat here, watching.

She smiled at them. "You could go in, you know?" she teased.

"We don't belong in the mermaid category," Bernie said. He was a big, burly man with a huge gut that they were working to reduce, and he was missing both legs. But they were missing very high up, so prosthetics would not be easy, if even possible.

She just smiled and said honestly, "With that tummy of yours, I'm sure you'd float anyway."

He grinned at her. "Like a beached whale or a turtle," he said.

She laughed. "Have you already had dinner?"

He patted his belly. "What do you think?" he asked. "You know me. When there's food, I'm never late."

She smiled, looked over at Stan beside him and said, "How are you doing? Surprised you are aren't still downstairs with the animals."

Stan, the vet, just smiled and gave her a tired nod. "I'm fine," he said. "Long day."

"Surgery?"

"Yes, plus I got two female cats and about eight kittens in today. The kittens aren't old enough to be fixed yet," he said, "but we did the moms, and then we had to round up fosters for the kittens. But everyone had to be chipped and inspected and examined and fixed," he said. "Fixed as in shots and ears checked, and a couple had ear infections."

She nodded. "Kind of sounds like my day," she said. "Hannah is sick for the second day now, and I'm just worn out doing double shifts."

"That's the thing, isn't it?" Stan said. "We can do everything just fine from Monday to Friday, bumping along quite happily with a regular workload, but then something happens, and our workload doubles."

She chuckled. "That's about it," she said. "In my case, staffing issues. I know Dani was trying to get somebody in temporarily to help but wasn't having luck. Then Hannah thought she'd be back today, but she didn't make it. But if she's not here tomorrow …"

"A pretty nasty flu is going around the place," Stan said. "If she caught that, she could be down for a week."

"A week?" Meredith cried out in mock horror. "If that's the case," she said, "I'll need Dani to get someone in to help. It's okay for a day or two, but, after that, it gets to be an issue."

"Of course it does," Stan said. "I was wondering about getting a second vet in here."

"You mean, until Aaron comes?"

"Exactly," he said with a grin, "and that, of course, will still be a few years out."

"True. Neither of our issues have an easy answer."

"Yours shouldn't be that hard to solve. Maybe you can talk to Dani after dinner," Stan said. "You're looking pretty tired."

There was such concern in his voice that she smiled at him and collapsed on the chair beside him. "I am," she said.

"Just work?"

She shot him a veiled look and shrugged.

He nodded. "I heard something about you and Gregory."

"Gossip travels fast around here," she said with a half smile, wishing he didn't know anything about it, but, of course, he did.

"Exactly," he said, "the gossip is notorious. But remember that we're all friends. Nobody wants to see you hurt."

"Might be a little late for that," she said. "Well, maybe five years late."

At that, Bernie wheeled away in this chair, calling back, "Private stuff. I'll leave you two alone."

"Thanks," she called out. She looked over at Stan and said, "It's hard to see Gregory and not wonder about the 'what ifs' in life. We've never mentioned our history. It's like a great big black hole that neither of us wants to get sucked into."

"Understandable. You don't know where a conversation like that will leave you. Still, you need to know where you stand inside first. If you can't determine that, then any further conversations would just confuse the issue. Learn what's in your heart, then find out what's in his. A lot of time has passed, and he's been through a rough time."

Stan stared out at the open deck. "He's lost a lot in his life. Not only his career but his health. He has years to recover and faces an uncertain future. He also lost you. And, although we're sorry for what he's been through, we can't do anything but help support this next part of his journey. He's stronger than he knows. You have to be too." Stan's piercing gray eyes locked onto hers as he said in a low tone, "Particularly if you want to keep him in your life."

"I know that mentally, but I still want to rail at him that, if he'd chosen me over the military way back when, then he wouldn't be in this situation. Yet I also know that would be the worst thing I could do, denying him what makes him *him*. Yet it hurts me so to see him suffering," she said, her shoulders sagging, "He's struggling, like really struggling sometimes."

"Everyone here does," Stan said, his voice still low so it wouldn't carry across to others around.

"I didn't want to see him go off to war again," she muttered. "I feel very selfish about it now, but I know I couldn't have lived with the constant fear and worry about him getting hurt. Even after he left, I still worried and felt fear. It took a long time to stop doing that." She waved a hand toward the rehab center sprawled around them. "And then to see him here like this?" She shook her head. "I know it's selfish, but I'm glad I wasn't there at the time. Yet I feel bad that I wasn't there for him."

"It would have been incredibly difficult," he said. "At least at this stage, you're seeing him already on the mend. You're seeing him on the road to recovery."

She nodded. "That's it exactly," she said. "I've seen him turn the corner, and I know that it's still hard for him, and, of course, there's added pain because of our own breakup. But, at the same time, it is showing me a side of him that I'd never seen before. I've seen men come here broken and, at the end of their stay, stand up and walk forward into their new lives, making me feel so proud to have been a part of their journey. To watch them step into their futures, when they didn't actually think they had one when they arrived.

"Most arrived broken, hating their lives. Their hearts had been devastated at what had happened to them. Very few are happy and upbeat. And I mean, very few. They're challenged here. They're given tasks and end goals, and yet, through it all, they learn abilities and gain strength and find an inner sense of who they really are. And, in a way, I feel like I missed something very important for Gregory from the time that he was injured until now. Because he was in much better shape than a lot of people when first checking in here," she finished.

"I don't know him all that well," Stan said, "but he appears to be fairly well-adjusted. And that's a surprise. Of course, we have lots of that here, but, as you said, he came in already in really good shape."

"And yet, our rehab has been a shock for him too. I think he became a little too complacent, thinking he already had this. I'm not sure his last VA center was the best place for him. He's one of those guys who can fool you into thinking that he's doing everything, and it's all working well, but he's actually taking shortcuts. So some of the very important steps that are necessary weren't taken, and now, well, you know what our PT guys are like. Shane won't let Gregory off the hook at all."

Stan chuckled. "No, Shane is quite a hard character, but he's fair."

"He's beyond fair," she said. "But he's also extremely good at what he does, and he already worked out Gregory's character on the first day. It is unfortunate though that, between the two of them, Gregory was overworked from his very first PT session, so that he was quite sore that night and into the next day. The thing is, he wasn't in anywhere as bad a shape as I've seen time and time again. But, for Gregory, I think he was more than shocked that he was in such poor condition as to not survive his first PT session with Shane. And that's not easy for Gregory to accept."

"Even harder," Stan said, nodding his head, "Gregory arrived with a false self-confidence. Shane abruptly woke him up from that to see where Gregory really was, and now he'll have to work."

"But, at the end of it," she said, "he will be where he wanted to be."

"And yet, something about that concerns you."

"I think I'm holding him back." Meredith sighed.

"What's your relationship like right now?"

"Professional," Meredith said. "I'm keeping it that way. We haven't discussed five years ago. We're ignoring it, but that means it's always there between us."

"And why is that?"

"I don't want to get in the way of the work he has to do here. When he first arrived, and we were a little friendlier, he didn't seem to think he had any work to do, so he was much more relaxed. But now it's different, as if he's got more locked up inside."

"Of course he has, because he has a true challenge to face. It's not something you can help him with, and you're right. Maybe in that instance, you'll actually feel his pain because he knows he has to do this, and he has to do it well. And, on top of that, you're there watching him. No matter whether it's as an ex-lover or as an old friend, no one wants to come up short."

At that, she stared at Stan. "In what way would he come up short?"

"Well, think about it," Stan said, as if it was blatantly obvious. "Five years ago he was whole and physically fit—and God only knows what else you saw in him—but he isn't those things anymore."

"No," she said slowly, thinking about it. "He used to

have a big smile and a huge sense of humor. But what hasn't changed is he's still strong, loyal, and committed."

"But those are what he would consider as *soft skills*. You know those job applications where you have to give your actual skills, but they want those *other* skills? Right now Gregory's looking for the measurable *real* skills—the ability to walk, the ability to be independent, to look after his own physical needs. He wants to know that he has a purpose in his life and that he can hold a job and can support a family." Stan smiled sadly at her. "No matter what the other person in the relationship is doing, it's always important that the men know that they can handle looking after their family. Women can become the major moneymaker. They can become the CEOs. They can become all kinds of things in this world," he said, "but it'll never change that a man wants to know he can be strong enough, capable enough to be the breadwinner."

"I guess the men are still hunter-gatherers at heart, aren't they?" she mused.

"We so are, and, considering we're both exhausted"—he grinned—"why don't you quickly go get changed, as much as I like the view, and we'll get dinner."

"How about I just throw on my sundress?" she said. She picked hers up from where she'd dropped it to the side with her towel and tossed it over her head, letting it float lightly over her body. She reached out a hand and said, "Come on. Let's go eat."

He reached up, grabbed it, squeezed her fingers and let her hand go. "Let's go." As they walked over to the edge, he said, "Don't look now, but somebody's been watching us for the last twenty minutes or so."

"I saw him," she said with a smile. "Do you think us

holding hands bothered him?"

"Absolutely," he said. "Which is why I dropped yours. Now let's eat."

IT WAS HARD to watch somebody who you cared about being friendly with another man. The handclasp was one thing, but at least it didn't last too long. The thing that bothered Gregory the most was the fact that it was obvious Meredith and Stan were close. But then, why wouldn't they be? They'd both worked at Hathaway House for years; they were bound to be friends. Gregory wondered painfully if that was all they were.

There was an obvious age difference between them, but it wasn't so much as to raise eyebrows. Meredith had always been mature for her age, and she was absolutely perfect, so, of course, every man in town wanted her. The thing was, she had chosen Gregory at one time, and he'd been so honored and so delighted, … until it came time for him to leave. He hadn't come up against that issue before because he hadn't really cared enough before.

But, with Meredith, everything had changed, and it had hurt big-time. And how could he even begin to contemplate a relationship with her now? She'd already seen him when he had been so much more, when he had walked away from her, so why would she want anything to do with him now?

Yet he was here, full of hope, winging it on a kiss and a prayer.

Honestly, it was heartbreaking. He knew he shouldn't be even thinking about it like that, but it wasn't easy. As much as he wanted it and was delighted and had actively taken a path that would have put Meredith right in front of him, it was hard to know what to do next, especially with the current rude awakening to the truth about his physical condition.

Hathaway House had a lot more to offer than he had ever expected.

She deserved so much more. If he was smart, he would have just walked away from the military years ago, and he'd have spent the last five years with her. Not only would he have had the last five years but he'd be whole now because he wouldn't have been blown up by the damn IED.

He stared out at the pool, knowing that Stan and Meredith would come upstairs and would walk past him at any moment. As they approached, she smiled at him, but Stan asked, "Have you eaten yet, Gregory?"

He looked up in surprise. "Actually I have," he said. "I was just thinking about going for a swim to help digest some of the food I shoved down there."

"Just make sure you wait a little bit, please," she cautioned.

Of course, always the nurse, he thought. The two of them walked past and headed to the cafeteria. Gregory wondered if an invitation would have been in the offering from her.

He moved toward the water. He had on his shorts and knew he could make his way in the pool, yet he couldn't force himself now that he was here. He had wanted to get out. He could have gone up and had dessert or something with them. They'd offered a branch of friendship, and instead, he'd been churlish and refused. He deserved to be alone right now. As he sat here, frowning, he turned to look up to see Meredith standing on the top step, looking at him.

She frowned, and he frowned right back.

"Do you want company?" she asked him.

Immediately his back stiffened, and he shook his head. "I'm fine," he said, and she quickly disappeared.

He groaned and quickly pulled off his T-shirt. He put his wheelchair alongside the ladder to get into the pool, hit the brakes on it, stood and helped himself into the water. As soon as the first wave splashed over his head, he could feel some of his tension easing. Now he was just miserable, and, every time he saw her, he felt like he said the wrong thing. And that wasn't fair to her, and it surely wasn't the reason he came here.

Putting some of his muscles to use, he swam laps, trying not to roll with his uneven leg movements and to stay straight. It didn't take too long to get caught up in the natural rhythm, and, as soon as he did, his stiffness left. Once he did a few more laps and calmed his breathing, he lowered himself in the water.

Shane had had a hard talk with him today. Gregory hadn't in any way realized he was doing it, but Shane had taken him to task for not showing up for the job. Gregory had been hurt and insulted at the time, but then, when Shane explained about how Gregory was putting up a front and telling them everything was fine but was only giving about seventy percent because he was sore, Gregory could see what Shane was talking about.

It wasn't his usual way to act, but Gregory realized that the other rehab center had let him get away with a lot, whereas Shane wouldn't let him get away with anything. Gregory knew that he would thank Shane for it later, but right now it felt brutal.

Gregory didn't know how long he swam. It was hard to

keep track. But, when he finally stopped, instead of feeling exhausted, he felt energized. His body hummed with joy; his muscles swelled with pleasure. He pulled himself up beside the wheelchair and just sat here. It was such a beautiful way to end a day, and he knew he'd sleep so much better.

But, of course, he hadn't thought about a towel. He looked around for one to grab and saw Meredith walking toward him, a towel in her hand. She held it out to him. Taking it, he muttered, "Thanks," and quickly dried his face. "Are you done eating already?" he asked, still drying his hair and not looking at her.

"Yes," she said. "Stan got called back to an emergency."

"Ah," he said.

"What does that mean?"

He shrugged. "Sorry that your dinner date was cut short."

An awkward silence followed for a moment, and then she crouched beside him. "Stan is a good friend," she said, looking Gregory in the eyes. "Shane is a good friend. Many other males here are also my good friends. You'll see me sharing a meal with them, many times probably," she said. "We're part of a very large family here, and it's very peaceful, comfortable. When I have something I need to talk out, I can pick any one of them, and I know that they'll just let me vent. They won't tell me how to fix the problem. They won't tell me what to do. They'll just listen, so that I can get some of it off my chest."

He nodded slowly. "I'm sorry. I didn't mean to be childish."

"No," she said, straightening. "But it's obvious that something about my dinner with Stan bothered you, and it's something we have to talk about."

Immediately he shook his head. "No," he said, "we don't have to at all."

"Yes," she said firmly. "We do."

"Well, not today," he said. "I don't think I can handle more today."

"Well, I agree with you there," she said. "I've been doing double-duty for several days, and I'm exhausted. I had a hard swim earlier, and now I've just eaten, so I'm heading back to my place. I'll see you in the morning." She turned, walked alongside the pool, picked up a towel that he hadn't even realized was there on the back of a chair, threw it over her shoulder and disappeared.

She was right; they did need to talk. But he was also right in that it didn't need to be today. He was the one who would need some time to work up what he wanted to say. Because really, what could he say? *Sorry* seemed awfully useless now.

Chapter 9

I T WAS NOON the next day when she finally sat back and looked up to see Dani walking in, a smile on her face.

"You've done really, really well," Dani said. "I'm so sorry about the staffing shortage, but I just heard from Hannah, and she'll be back in tomorrow."

Meredith gave a huge sigh of relief. "Good," she said. "I've been trying to handle it, but it's getting away from me."

"Understood. Hanna will see if she can get in to do an hour or two today and maybe catch up on some of the paperwork for you, but she wants to avoid the patients until she's a hundred percent clear of flu symptoms."

"Absolutely," Meredith said. "It's always the rule, isn't it? The last thing we want to do is spread any germs around this place."

"Exactly. Now I told her, that if she wasn't feeling up to it, not worry. The paperwork would still be there tomorrow."

"It always is," Meredith said with a heavy sigh. "It always is."

"I am interviewing for more staff. I'm sorry I'm not further along on that process."

Meredith nodded and waved off her comments.

Dani looked at her and asked, "Are you doing okay with Gregory?"

Meredith gave an irritable shrug. "I am. It's not that easy, and I'm not exactly sure what I'm supposed to do, as we do need to talk and clear the air, but I can't seem to find the right time."

"You know you have to pick your time carefully, right?" Dani asked softly, checking to make sure nobody else was listening to their private conversation.

"I know," she said. "I was hoping to avoid him, and then I pushed the issue last night." She sighed. "But he said we couldn't talk yesterday, and I was too tired anyway."

"Maybe have a talk with Shane first, and see if Gregory's adapting well. The last thing we want to do is cause a relapse."

At that, she winced. "Right, that would push the conversation back a couple more weeks."

"Maybe just try to be friends for now?" Dani asked curiously. "I'm not sure what it is you're trying to do, whether you want to go back to him or not."

"I know. It's kind of hard. I want to be friendly. We can't go back to what we had because, well, ... I just don't think we can," she said honestly. "Maybe something better though. But I don't even know if I like him right now." She had a sad smile on her lips as she spoke. "I don't really recognize him."

"So you know what this is," Dani said. "This is the time to get to know each other, like really get to know him, to see who he is inside, not just the outside."

"That's all we ever see here, isn't it? So many are broken. So many are working on becoming better," Meredith said. "We see so much of the inner person all the time here."

"And I think it's very different here for him," Dani said. "And he needs time. He needs space."

"And that's exactly what I was trying to give him," Meredith said. "But it's not easy being his primary care nurse, which throws us together. Often."

"I know," Dani said with the sweetest smile. "I do understand." With a lopsided grin, the two women exchanged hugs. "Now let's hope Hannah comes this afternoon," Dani said as she headed out. "That will help relieve some of your workload. I really appreciate you stepping up while she's been down."

"You know me," Meredith said. "The super-responsible type." And, with a flippant look, she grabbed her tablet. "Speaking of which, I have to go."

"Don't avoid him," Dani called out to her retreating back. "Just treat him like one of the regular guys."

"Oh, he is," Meredith threw back, with a saucy grin, turning to see Dani. "Just with one big difference."

Dani chuckled. "And that difference, of course, is everything."

Meredith thought about that as she kept going because a lot of truth was in that statement. She already knew who he was in one way; this situation would just add another layer to her knowledge. Maybe this time she would make a better decision, and so could he.

GREGORY WORKED AS he'd never worked in his life. His water-based military training had been absolutely brutal, and, at the time, he'd cursed his way through it, finding strength in the brotherhood around him to make it through. But right now, he didn't think anything could possibly be worse than what he was doing. And when he finally collapsed, his body shaking, Shane squatted beside him and said, "Remember. On a scale of one to ten, you are to tell me when you're at a six."

Gregory glared at him. "And why would I do that?" he asked. "If I keep giving my body a chance to quit before it's done, it'll never push the level of achievement higher."

"Because, when you go past a six out of ten," Shane said patiently, "you're pushing your body well past the point where it can recover easily. And, instead of helping your body, you're hurting it. You're putting it into a stressful position it can't recover from easily. That's not what we want."

"I want to get better," Gregory snapped. "I want to be healthy again. I want to be strong again."

Shane straightened, looked at him and said, "What you really want is to turn back time to be who you were before. That's not happening." He closed his folder and picked up his tablet. "We're done here for the day. I suggest you either get back to your room and have a shower or maybe do some time at the pool." And he turned and walked out.

Gregory, still writhing with anger, wanted to follow him and yell at him and scream and rail at the injustices of life. Instead, he picked up the weights and did ten more reps, feeling the sweat pour off his body until he couldn't lift the weights again.

He groaned and collapsed on the mat and just laid here. He thought he was done being angry about his current life; he thought he was done being frustrated and hating his world. And yet, coming here, seeing Meredith, seeing her happy and joyful and laughing with all the other men made him realize just how much he wanted to be that man again.

But he wouldn't *ever* be that man again.

She was a nurse. She saw more broken men than he'd ever seen in his life. And he didn't give a damn because it was his life, his broken body he wanted her to see, but he didn't want her to see it as it was today; he wanted her to see it as it had been. Only his body wouldn't be that fit again.

And, to his humiliation, he could feel tears burning up in the corner of his eyes. He immediately squeezed his eyes closed to stop the tears from leaking out. The last thing he wanted was to be caught crying like a baby. When he'd laid on the battlefield in pieces, he had bawled in agony. But then every man around him—except for those dead friends whose eyes he could see staring skyward—were crying too. There was nothing like that horrible sense of waking up and realizing how vastly his world had changed.

For a long time, he'd wished he'd died on that field. But, in his last rehab center—for whatever reason—he'd been fine there. He'd been doing okay, until he'd come here, and they'd taken all that false reality away from him. They'd taken that mirage that he was comfortable living in, and they'd showed him where he *really* was and what he really could do—or not do.

And what he really looked like beside the rest of the men in the world.

Deep down, Gregory knew it wasn't Hathaway House's fault, but he wanted to rail at them and make it their fault. He knew as much as anything it was the fact that Shane wasn't a pushover, like his other therapist had been.

It was also Meredith's presence here. He'd come here specifically to see her, but he'd expected to still be that king of the walk. That same confident, capable person who had arrived on the first day at Hathaway House. Instead, he was more broken than he'd ever been, and he couldn't show her that confident person anymore because he didn't exist, had never existed. He was just someone Gregory had made up to make it through life when the reality inside him was that he hadn't even begun to heal.

At the sound of footsteps, he quickly sat up and struggled over to his wheelchair.

He was just hopping in and collapsing down when a woman's voice called from the doorway, "Are you okay?"

He mustered up a smile, nodded and said, "Just fine, heading back for a shower now."

The woman in scrubs nodded and walked away. He thought her name was Shannon. He again wondered if having Meredith around was helping or hurting him. He wanted her to be the goal at the end of the day, but he also knew he couldn't make that his goal, as it was something out of his own control. But just because he knew that didn't mean that he wanted that to be the truth. He wanted something so much better for himself. And Hathaway House was giving it to him, just not the way he expected.

Exhausted and depressed like he hadn't been in months, he made his way back to his room slowly. He had a shower, taking his time because he was so tired. As he let the heat roll down his sore muscles, he knew that he had pushed it too far. He had refused to listen to Shane once again, and he would pay for it tonight. Maybe even sooner than that.

Back at his bed, he took several muscle relaxants, and, rather than struggling to stay awake, he laid down, pulled a sheet over himself and closed his eyes.

Chapter 10

WHEN MEREDITH GOT to work the next morning, she found Dani waiting for her. In a serious voice, Dani said, "I need to talk to you."

Surprised, she nodded. "Here or in your office?"

"In my office." Worried, Meredith followed Dani to her private office, and she closed the door and motioned at the chair, just saying, "Be seated."

She got doubly worried. "Have I done something wrong?"

Dani immediately shook her head. "No, you haven't. However, it goes back to you and Gregory."

"Oh, in what way?"

"Some of the others on his team feel that your relationship is impacting his ability to heal."

Meredith sagged in the chair. "And I was trying to avoid him, other than doing my job, hoping that, if I wasn't around all the time, it would make it easier for him."

"I think we need to make it a little more than that," Dani said. "He hasn't requested this, but I'll be interested to see if he says anything about it. I'd like you to switch your care to exclude him. And I will ask one of the other nurses to pick up his room as part of their roster."

Meredith could feel a little bit of her shrinking inside yet again. "Okay," she said slowly. "Is that really necessary?"

"No, maybe not," Dani said honestly. "Shane says that Gregory's angry at himself, and he's pushing himself well past the point of normal. Shane thinks that's because a certain amount of Gregory's rage has come back because he's not where he was before he was injured, and Shane's wondering if it's because Gregory can see you around here."

"I didn't tell Shane about our history," Meredith said honestly, "but I probably should have."

"I told him," Dani said. "You know we can't keep something like that a secret from our patient's team. But Shane thinks that Gregory wants to impress you, that he wants you to see him as he was, and so he's pushing himself, and what we're heading toward is a complete breakdown."

Meredith chewed on her bottom lip, worried. "We've certainly seen that in a few of our cases," she said, "at least ones with that much rage still in them."

"Exactly," Dani said. "We understand the rage. What Gregory has to do is get past it and get to the acceptance part. And I don't know at what point in time we'll see the blowout. I don't want you to set it off, and I don't want him to use you as a catalyst. This needs to be his fight for his own healing and not because of what he lost and thinks he can never regain."

Meredith reached up, not surprised to feel tears dripping down her cheeks. Dani reached for a box of tissues and held it out to her. She pulled out one and dabbed at the corner of her eyes. "I had convinced myself that it would be easy to see him, and then I would be totally over him," she said. "But I'm not. And to see how hard he's working, to see what he's trying to do, ... I know he came here overconfident and had that knocked out of him in his very first session with Shane. But it was hard to see him drop down to no confidence."

"And again, we've seen it time and time again," Dani said gently. "He has to get through this yawning pit of despair so he can come out the other side and crawl back up to the light again. You know perfectly well he can get back to being the person he was when he arrived. But the person he was upon arrival wasn't real. That was fake. That was Gregory's fantasy, his imagination. No way is he as strong as he thought he was. And all Shane has done is show him that he was hiding his defects. Defects that would have caught up with Gregory sooner or later. Those weaknesses are what will put him back into a wheelchair in a few years."

Meredith gave Dani a watery smile. "The thing is, we both know that. But when it becomes personal ..."

"Which is why I want to remove the personal element," Dani said. "Let's try it for a week, and see if he notices."

"And it will be heartbreaking if he doesn't notice," Meredith said brokenly. There wasn't much else she could say, so she nodded and said, "Am I to avoid him in the rest of the place too? I hate to make it obvious like that because he will wonder if it's my decision."

"I don't think that's necessary," Dani said, speaking slowly as she thought about it. "We don't want him to think you're doing that. If he asks you what happened, just tell him that I changed your roster."

Meredith stood. "Okay, I can do that."

Dani looked up at her and smiled. "You're being very brave."

"I don't feel very brave," she said. "Since he arrived, I feel like I've been on nothing but a roller coaster ride. It's been very rough."

"I know," Dani said. "Believe me. I do know." And, of course, that just referenced Dani's crazy up and down relationship at the beginning with Aaron, another patient and a longtime friend of Dani's.

Meredith smiled, gave her a hug and said, "At least in your case you are at a point where you no longer have all those doubts."

"No," Dani said with a smile, "thankfully I'm well past that."

"When's the wedding?" Meredith teased.

Dani's face flushed. "Not sure," she said, "but we are talking about setting a date."

"Well, you know that everybody here will want to be part of it," she said with a laugh. "So you better plan for that too."

"Absolutely," Dani said chuckling. "But that just adds to the logistics issue."

"No, not at all," Meredith said. "Get a minister and have the ceremony here. And for the reception? You know the kitchen will want to handle that. Whoever is here at the time gets to attend, and, other than that, it's really not about anybody else. It's all about you and Aaron."

"True enough," Dani said. "We'll think about it."

"I'm sure you do nothing but." Meredith smiled.

"Well, it is kind of nice," Dani replied. "As you said, I already know that we're together, and that makes a world of difference. I don't get to see him anywhere near enough, and, for a couple years, that's the way it'll be, but after that? Well, it's a whole different story."

"Do you think Stan is seriously interested in working with Aaron?"

Dani beamed. "He can't wait for him to get here. He's needed a partner for a long time. Whenever Aaron is off, he comes down and helps anyway. He'll do part of his practicum with Stan as it is."

"Now that sounds perfect," Meredith said warmly. "I'm really happy for you."

And, on that note, she turned and walked out. She might be happy for Dani, but Meredith still had a long way to go to get her own life together. She could only hope it happened a little sooner rather than later because this was just too hard. She went to bed thinking about Gregory, and she woke up thinking about him. How fair was it to know that now she wasn't even supposed to work with him? That had been the one light in her day. So many times in a day she got to check up on him. And now, ... well, even that was gone. She understood the reasoning, and a week wasn't a long time to see if it would make a difference or not. But it would seem like forever, ... at least to her.

SEVERAL DAYS LATER Gregory finally asked the question on his mind. At first, he hadn't been sure, but now too much time had passed. "Why did Meredith ask to be removed from my team?" Gregory asked Shane bluntly.

Shane stopped what he was doing, crouched so he could look at his face and then said, "What are you talking about?"

"She's not part of my team anymore."

"I don't know," Shane said. "Doesn't mean it was her choice though."

"Of course it was," Gregory scoffed. "Obviously she doesn't like to see who I am now."

"I think you're doing Meredith a great injustice," Shane said. "Of all the things I know about her, she sees people very, very clearly."

At that, Gregory closed his mouth and went back to work. He didn't like these exercises at all. They were working on one of the strips down his back that had been badly mangled. Part of it was still there; part of it was damaged, and the scar tissue kept pulling. Shane kept working on it. Softening it, loosening it, telling Gregory that they could ease some of these knots and get it to stretch out properly. But, so far, Gregory didn't believe him. It just seemed like pain upon pain with absolutely no joy at the end of the day.

It'd been four days since he'd seen Meredith.

"Do you think she's avoiding me?" he muttered, not letting the subject go.

"No," Shane said firmly. "She's incredibly busy. We've had a lot of new people come on board, and I think she's just a swamped as everybody else is in here. Now, focus."

At that, Gregory shut up because he didn't have a job himself right now. And that's what Meredith's position here was—it was a job for her—unlike him, who was here twenty-four hours a day, whereas she didn't have to be. She could have a life outside of this place.

When he was finally done, his hands were shaking, but unfortunately, he was afraid it was a buildup of rage inside, a rage that had been building slowly for the last few days. He didn't know what to do about it, but he was terrified he would lash out and hurt somebody. He closed his hands into fists and clenched them tightly, trying to let out some of that energy. When he opened them again, Shane stared at him calmly but knowingly.

"You've got to let it blow, you know?"

Immediately Gregory shook his head. "I can't." His tone was harsh. "I might hurt someone."

"Maybe," Shane replied. "But you can't keep it inside."

"Why not?" he snapped. "It's what I have done so far."

"Sure," he said, "but a rage like that is not healthy, and it's holding you back. I get that you're not who you were. I get that life dished you something you didn't want to see. … I even get that you had choices that you could have made before that would have changed where you are right now, … but none of it matters. Because you can't go back. You can't change it. You can't fix it. All you can do right now is play the hand you've been dealt."

Gregory knew everything Shane said was true, but it didn't matter. Gregory glared at his hands, and he could feel the vibration starting deep inside. "I need to go to the pool or something," he said, his voice thick.

"Ever used a punching bag?"

He lifted his head, stared at Shane and frowned.

"If you haven't, now might be a good time to try it. If you have, I've got one down in one of the other rooms."

"What kind?"

"Get in your wheelchair, and I'll take you," Shane said. "You need an outlet, and you need it fast."

Once he was in the wheelchair, Shane grabbed the handles and pushed, not even giving Gregory a chance to go on his own power. Shane took him past more rooms, then brought him to a room he'd never been in before. Shane opened it up to reveal a beautiful hardwood floor with several hanging balls and punching bags. Gregory got up, grabbed his crutches mounted on the back of his wheelchair, hobbled over and said, "It's not exactly something I can do with crutches."

"No," Shane replied. "But I do have this over here."

Gregory walked over to see a generic prosthetic, probably useless for most cases, but it would give him the ability to stand. They quickly strapped it on, and he took several experimental steps. "Even this is so much better than crutches."

"Your prosthetic is on the way," Shane said. "We took the molds. We don't know if the stump has healed enough yet to support it, but we thought with extra socks and maybe a bit of a cushioning, you'd be okay with it. This, however, isn't it. This is just something for you to get around with for right now."

Gregory nodded. He stared at his good fist. That same damn rage sat in his gut, burning a hole. "I didn't even realize how angry I was," he said. "It's a red haze that's building."

"Because you're not acknowledging it," Shane said. "You're keeping it stuffed inside, and it'll just hurt you. It'll eat you from the inside out, and it will demand an outlet. Whether you like it or not, it will insist on coming out. It has to. Have you ever used a punching bag before?"

Although Shane had asked the question before, Gregory hadn't answered him. He nodded. "I'm not the best at it though. My hands won't handle much."

At that, Shane walked over to the side and picked up two gloves. He helped strap them on Gregory's hands, and, when they were secure, Shane said, "I'll hold the bag, and I want you to pound into it as much as you want and as hard as you want. Release as much of that anger as you need to in order to get your mind back on getting you in shape. Are you ready to release? You've got a ways to go yet in your therapy, and you're making it a very slow, arduous journey. We already need a couple months. But, if you don't deal with this, it'll take six months instead. I don't know that I can get you as high or as far or as fast if you can't let this out."

Shane may have said all that only to shut him up, but Gregory's instinct to reach up and pound into that bag was instinctive, and he struck out, pounding the bag once, twice, and then he couldn't stop. With Shane holding it somewhat steady and taking the force of the blunted blows, Gregory beat on that bag as if it were every damn commander who had made a wrong decision. For every wrong decision Gregory had made. For his body not recovering as fast as it had been blown up. For everything and everyone he blamed for his life and his fate and his so-called karma. For every damn thing in his world that had gone so very wrong.

Gregory just kept pounding ... and pounding ... and pounding ... and pounding, until finally, he could hear somebody's voice in the background. He slowly collapsed to his knees. He wrapped his arms around his chest and started to sob. His humiliation was complete when he heard another voice. Then both disappeared. All of it disappeared into the silence around him, and he realized that Shane had moved whoever it was out of the room and stood outside in the hallway with them.

Gregory sat here, feeling his body completely collapse in on itself. So much pain. So much anger. So much torment in his soul. It was as if there was no freedom, no way out.

As he had always done before, he slammed a lid down on his emotions and collapsed, so he lay on the floor and stared up. The tears were tears of exhaustion at this point in time, and he knew he couldn't even unlace his gloves. They were darn hard to get in and out of normally, but alone it was almost impossible. Especially today, ... right now ...

He took several deep, calming breaths, trying to find a center that would allow him to move forward in life. But he couldn't even sit up. How the hell would he go anywhere? Finally he heard the door open, and Shane walked back in.

"How do you feel now?"

"Empty," he croaked as he reached up one gloved fist. "Could you help me with these, please?" His voice was low and quiet. *Empty.*

Shane quickly unlaced them and tugged them off. He set them aside, then brought the wheelchair over. "I would suggest that pool now to finish off your workout, then a bit of time in the hot tub."

Gregory shook his head. "No," he said, "the only thing I want to do is go to my room and stay there."

"That's the worst thing you can do."

"It doesn't matter if it's the worst thing or not. I don't have the energy to go to the pool. I don't have the energy to do anything. I'd like to go back to my room and be alone now."

Shane hesitated. "You know something? I think the answer to that is no." He helped him into the wheelchair, then, without giving him a chance, grabbed the handles on the back.

"I don't want to go anywhere public," Gregory snapped in outrage. He tried to grab the wheels, but Shane was too strong, too fast, refusing to listen. "And I definitely don't want to go to the cafeteria."

"Doesn't matter what you want at this point," Shane said, his voice and tone brooking no argument. "Your therapy session isn't done."

"It is done," he snapped. "And I want to go back to my room. You can't force me to do anything." Hating it, his voice rose like a truculent child.

"Yes," Shane said, "I can. You'll have to get up off that chair to stop me."

Gregory was so angry. Again. Where had that anger come from? How could there possibly be any more anger? He was exhausted; his body was pummeled from the therapy. Then he'd beaten his hands to death in the gloves, and his shoulders were killing him. There shouldn't have been any more anger, but it was rising yet again in another red wave.

"I'll have you fired for this," he roared. He knew he was attracting attention, but, shit, he couldn't stop himself.

Shane chuckled. "If it was that easy to fire me," he said, "I would have been fired a long time ago. I've been dealing with guys like you for over a decade," he said, "and I do understand a lot about it, and I understand that layers and layers and layers of rage are inside. The sooner we can deal with them, the better we all are."

"Didn't I get enough out already?" Gregory snapped. "You not happy with your job? Is that what this is? Are you just angry because you don't see another little successful check in a box beside your name?" he asked snidely. He hated the way he was acting, but he didn't know how to stop it. It was just too unbelievable. Suddenly they were at the pool level.

He glared at the beautiful gleaming water, even though part of him desperately wished to be swimming in it. But he didn't want Shane to know that.

Except Shane had absolutely no intention of giving him the upper hand. He hit the edge of the wheelchair with the ladder and locked down the wheels to the chair. He walked in front of Gregory and said, "You go in voluntarily, or I'll pick you up and put you in."

Gregory glared at him and said, "No way in hell you'll get away with doing that."

Shane nodded, scooped him up underneath his arms,

and then, with a quick flip, tossed him into the deep end of the pool. Gregory hit the water, and his outrage came in a scream of fury as he kicked and pounded and screamed underwater. Suddenly he came up, gasping for air, to find Shane already in the water beside him.

Gregory glared at him and said, "What kind of a sadistic move was that?"

"It was a good one," Shane said. "I haven't thrown a patient around in a few years, which is too damn bad as it's really cathartic."

"It's also not legal."

"Stop being such a crybaby, and listen to your therapist."

"Like hell," Gregory roared as he stroked away from him. There was something so damn calming, so peaceful and so good when doing that. But he was also exhausted. Four laps later, he found himself doing the breaststroke, trying to maintain his floating, and realizing that he'd burned out so much energy that it was all he could really do.

He rolled over onto his back and just floated, letting his body and mind relax. Without any warning, a huge sigh worked up from his belly and his chest. He could feel something inside him letting loose, a great big boulder that he'd been hanging onto. He didn't recognize it. He didn't know how, but, with whatever had happened this afternoon, he could just feel it pouring from his mouth and chest as he released heavy sigh after heavy sigh after heavy sigh.

And yet, again feeling tears in his eyes, he turned over to float facedown so that nobody could see. He didn't know what had just happened, but, for the first time in a long time, he felt a hell of a lot better.

But he'd be damned if he'd let Shane know that.

Chapter 11

A S THE WEEK went by, Meredith thought these were some of the worst days she'd ever experienced. Dani's request had been official, so Meredith avoided Gregory as much as she could. Of course, it was impossible to avoid him all the time, and she did not deliberately go out of her way to avoid him in public settings, like the cafeteria or the pool. However, she rarely caught a glimpse of him, and, when she did, it was always from a distance.

However, every time she did see him, her heart ached at the pain on his face. She understood that Shane was working him hard, but there was also a murmur of some kind of a breakthrough. And, for that, she was absolutely overjoyed. If it came because of her absence, that made her seriously sad, but, if that's what it took to get Gregory back on his feet, then that's what it took.

To keep her mind off of him, Meredith became super efficient and super busy. She kept herself occupied every moment of the day, until finally, Dani called her into her office to talk. Meredith plunked down on a nearby chair, her arms full of files and tablets. Looking at Dani, she raised an eyebrow. "What's up?"

"You," Dani replied bluntly. "Several of the staff members have noticed that you're very edgy, that you're working too hard and that it's obvious how you're stressed about something. The idea was to relieve the stress, not to increase it."

Her back stiff, she stared at Dani, trying to figure out what she was supposed to do now. "The idea was to reduce Gregory's stress, I believe, not mine." Then she winced at her cattiness. Finally, she sagged in place and said, "I can't stop thinking about him, and the only way I can avoid spending too much time doing that is if I stay busy. And, if I'm not busy, then I just wallow."

"Understood," Dani said gently. "And I do have an official word here from Shane saying that Gregory's not completely over it all yet, but he hit one of those walls and broke through it. A lot of Gregory's anger has been released from his soul. They're working on getting some more of it out, but Gregory has reached a turning point."

Meredith beamed. "I'm really glad to hear that," she said. "I'm really sorry it came because of my absence, but I understand."

"I'm not sure it came from your absence at all," Dani said. "In a way, actually it might very well have been *because* of your absence but for another reason. I think he was angry that you weren't there for him. Whether it was because he understands you didn't have a choice or not, I don't know. But that anger at what he perceived as a slight from you was enough anger to push him up and over the edge."

"Ouch," Meredith said. "So by me following your orders, it made him angry enough to blow, thus letting go of some of these issues?"

Dani nodded. "And that might be hard for you to accept," she said, "but you might want to consider the fact that this is probably exactly what he needed."

"So, now what?" Meredith asked quietly. "It's been a

week."

Dani nodded. "Shane's requested that you stay away for another, say, two or three days, maybe as long as another week. Then we'll bring you two together and see where Gregory's anger spikes again and how."

"Along with psychologists?"

"Maybe, if needed," Dani said with a serious tone to her voice. "The whole point of this is his healing."

"I know." It was on the tip of her tongue to ask what about *her* healing, except she wasn't the important one here. She was one of the staff, not one of the patients. And there was only so much that anybody could do in a situation like this.

"And I understand how hard it is for you," Dani said. "But remember that, when he's a whole person, it makes life a whole lot easier on everyone."

"Exactly," Meredith said, standing up. "Anything else?"

Dani shook her head. "No, you're free to go, but please, slow your pace down. Your absence did what we needed it to do, and you will get over this, and so will Gregory. You can both make up over this," Dani reiterated.

Meredith let her lips quirk upward into a semismile. "I hope so," she said, "because he's a good man, and I value his friendship."

"Are you friends?" Dani asked curiously, stretching back in her chair, her arms in her lap. "Did you ever get to that stage where you're actually friends too?"

"I thought we were getting there," she said, "but we haven't really had enough time. And, no, you're right, before it was much less of a friendship and more of a relationship."

"Exactly. So maybe take the time, once we pull the brakes off, to get to know him, know who he really is, and see if he's still the same person you fell in love with."

Meredith walked to the door, and she then turned. "The trouble is, I already know. As soon as I saw him again, I already knew I'd made the wrong decision last time. I just hadn't acknowledged it. Until I couldn't see him again." And she turned and walked away.

She headed back to the nurse's office and just stared at her monitor. There was absolutely nothing going well for her today. *Another two to three days.* She shook her head. "That'll be very painful."

"I know," a man said from the doorway.

She looked up to see Shane. She frowned at him. "I don't want Gregory to think that it was my choice to stay away."

"And we'll tell him eventually," he said. "But we had to spike that anger so we could find an outlet for it."

"And I understand that," she said. "At least in theory I do. But it hurts. I hate to think of him hurting because of something he perceives me to have done when I didn't."

Shane folded his arms across his chest. "I promise we'll fix it afterward," he said, trying to put her worries to rest.

She nodded and stared down at her paperwork. "Another two to three days?"

"If you could, yes, please."

"Of course. Anything for him."

As Shane retreated, he tossed back, "It'll go very fast."

She muttered to herself, "Not fast enough." She knew the damage had already been done no matter what they said, but it's what she had to deal with, and Gregory's health came first. That was her job. For the first time in a long time, she realized how much her job sucked at times. But there was no point in moaning about it, so she reburied herself in her work.

THERE WAS STILL no sign of Meredith. Gregory wondered if it was her choice or if she had been ordered to stay away. Maybe both. He'd been a pretty ugly sight these last few days, he admitted. He didn't know any other way to have it work, so he wasn't someone she should be around regardless. It's not like he was at this best. He didn't really know what he was doing yet because the slightest thing could set him off. When he mentioned it to Shane, he had nodded and said, "We need to get more of it out."

"I don't want to," Gregory said quietly. "I don't like seeing that part of my personality."

"Which is why it's even more important to release it all," Shane said, his tone equally low. "Particularly if there's anybody around here you want to spend time with. That anger is old. It's bitter, and it'll poison everything around you."

Instantly Gregory's face shut down. He looked around the room and said, "What are we doing next?" He watched Shane hesitate and then nod.

"Let's move on to the water exercises. I've wanted to give you some specific things to work on while you're there."

"Good enough," Gregory replied. "It's almost four o'clock anyway."

"So we'll spend a half hour going over some things in the water. Now I want you to practice this a minimum of three to five times a week, if you can."

"I don't even get to the pool that often," Gregory said.

"Well, from now on, we'll make it a part of your

workout. It's one of the best whole-body exercises that we can do for ourselves."

"Well, I guess these shorts I've got on are my swim shorts anyway," he said, "so let's go down." He led the way to the elevator, out to the patio, only to see Meredith leaning over the deck above. He feasted his eyes on her until someone called her away.

Without giving Shane any chance to *help* Gregory— particularly after the last time, when Shane had locked the wheelchair and threw Gregory in—he took a couple hops to the railing, being careful to not slip, and fell in. The water closing over his head wasn't the same kind of relief that he'd experienced last time, but then the last time had been so emotional that he'd been drained afterward. He'd even spent most of the last several evenings eating dinner in his room. Now this pool work would force him back in the public eye again, and he wasn't sure he was ready for it.

Gregory came back up slowly and floated. This time, Shane walked along the edge. He instructed Gregory to go through the paces of standard swimming techniques to see just where he was at.

Gregory shook his head and said, "I did this for a living." He swam like the dolphin he was, back and forth from one stroke to the other, rolling forward and backward and sideways. When he finally came to a stop, Shane grinned at him.

"Feels good, doesn't it?"

Gregory nodded. "It does. So, what is it you want me to do in here?"

They went over a series of exercises that seemed simple enough at first, but Gregory very quickly learned that *simple* with Shane was not simple because Gregory had to do it exactly as Shane said, and he wanted certain muscles isolated. No other muscle was allowed to come into play. And that was really hard as Gregory had found the gluteus maximus— or his butt—had a tendency to take over everything it possibly could.

Shane explained. "That's because it's the big stalwart muscle that knows it can handle this. It's always protecting and guarding the rest of the body. But, as such, the rest of the body gets to be weak and isn't gaining any strength, like it needs to be. So these exercises that seem like they're nothing will make a big difference."

Gregory trusted him so far. Shane had led him into the storm and then guided him safely back out again, so Gregory would certainly trust Shane as he went into the water and back out again. But it wasn't easy to sort through. As a matter of fact, it seemed like a lot of trouble, and for what? By the time Shane had explained exactly what to do and when to do it, Gregory felt his own body rebelling. Finally he stopped and said, "Six."

Shane assessed the truth of his words and the pain of the workout, then nodded. "Now it's dinnertime, if you care."

"Well, I care," Gregory replied. "It's just that I'll stay in the water for a bit. Feels like a little bit of energy needs to be broken down."

Shane studied his face for a long moment. "No more than another twenty minutes. We're not going back into the muscle-cramp scenario we slid into before."

Understanding, Gregory immediately headed back to swimming. As long as he focused on his laps, he could get his mind off Meredith. When he finally came to a stop, he wasn't tired, but all his senses had been on alert, making the swim not so relaxing. As he looked up and casually looked around, he still saw no sign of Meredith. She wasn't coming back.

He could feel his insides deflating. Had she left on purpose to avoid him? It seemed like that's what she had been doing these days. But then, looking sideways, he saw Shane and Meredith standing at the top of the stairs, talking—he hoped not about him. Because that would be humiliating. He knew that Meredith herself was very private and wouldn't want to be talked about, so he hoped that she would give him the same courtesy. He made his way to the side and, of course, realized too late that he had forgotten a towel.

He looked around and hopped up, standing on his one leg. He could walk if he had to, use his stump for balance for a moment or two, but it would just set him back from getting a prosthetic, so he sat down in his wheelchair, wet and all, and moved to where the towels were. There, he switched to the bench, took the towel, dried off his wheelchair and then proceeded to dry himself.

It was nice enough out that he wanted to just lie in the sun. He folded his towel, put it on the wheelchair and then wheeled over to one of the loungers, where he stretched out and closed his eyes. It had been a long time since he'd done something like this, and it felt good. He was starting to feel really good on the inside.

It wasn't anything like what he'd thought *good* actually felt like when he'd first arrived here because *this* felt like a holistic inside-out kind of good. He knew it didn't make any sense, and it was darn hard to explain, but it was helpful. And, with that, he closed his eyes and napped.

Chapter 12

MEREDITH LOOKED AT Gregory down below on the lounger. She didn't want him to sleep too long or to miss dinner or to get too burnt.

Shane leaned against the railing beside her. "You really care, don't you?"

"I do," she said. "I made a mistake five years ago with him. And I knew he was coming here, and I tried to prepare myself. But I honestly thought, after all this time, probably nothing was between us, but there certainly is on my side. But I didn't let myself believe it."

"I know it won't make you feel any better because of the enforced separation that we've requested, but he cares too."

"Oh, he cares," she said, "but I'm not sure it's the right kind of caring." She gave Shane a sad smile and continued, "I don't know if you're standing here to watch over him, but he could burn."

"I'll stay here and have a cup of coffee," he said. "I'm meeting up with a bunch of our new residents."

"Good. I'll get changed, have a shower and come back for dinner." She disappeared quickly. If it was the only way to stop Shane's conversation, then she'd take it. Back at her place, she realized she should have picked up a plate of dinner and brought it home with her; then she wouldn't have to worry about going back out there.

For a moment, she contemplated the idea of just staying in for the night and then decided she needed the social aspect too. She'd been working so hard these last few days that she'd isolated herself even more than usual. Forcing herself into shorts and a tank top with a light sweater, in case a breeze came up, she put on sandals and headed back outside.

She stopped along the pastures and smiled at the horses. Appie and Lovely were running across the field, absolutely delighted with the day.

Appie jumped and kicked, and the little baby llama tried to follow. Meredith laughed out loud, loving the mix of animals in nature. When something cold nudged her hand, she looked down to see Helga, the great big Newfoundland with the peg leg, beside her. She crouched and gave her a big hug. "Are you supposed to be out here on your own?" she chided. "Or is that the problem? You are out here on your own, and you're completely lost. Or lonely." She gave her a big cuddle and then straightened, brushing the dog hair off her, and walked toward the pool area, calling Helga to join her.

She looked up to see if Shane was still watching over Gregory, but he'd disappeared. That would mean Gregory was probably gone too, but then she saw him, still napping on a lounger. Helga was at her side the whole way. It was a problem trying to keep her out of the pool most of the time, and Dani, not wanting to have the poor dog suffer in the heat, especially with Helga's heavy coat of fur, had changed to a different filter system on the pool, so the animals could come in at times too. And just then, Helga got the idea, and she raced ahead and did a belly flop into the pool.

Meredith giggled and giggled, her cupped hands at her

mouth to not disturb Gregory's nap, while Helga swam back and forth. Then she hopped up the steps, stood at the top and gave an almighty shake, splattering water all over Gregory. He woke with a startled cry as he sat up to see Helga right beside him, shaking hard.

He looked at her, laughed and said, "There are easier ways to wake up."

"Maybe," Meredith said as she walked toward him. "But it's a fairly unique one, you must admit."

"Maybe not around this place," he said.

Helga walked closer to Gregory so she'd get a cuddle from him, and, as his hand came away completely coated in wet dog hair, he sighed. "This is definitely not the cleanest way to head in for dinner."

"And that's why there are outdoor showers, soap and a separate drainage system right over there." She pointed a few feet away from the pool.

He looked and smiled. "I don't think I even noticed that before." Getting up, he made his way to his wheelchair, rolled over where he could turn on a sprinkler head system and quickly washed up again. He looked at her and asked, "Are you going up for dinner?"

She laughed. "I'm starved, so, yes. You?"

"Maybe in a bit," he said, his tone turning more formal. "I've got to get changed first."

She nodded and immediately withdrew. "Enjoy," Meredith said. She scampered up the stairs as fast as she could. At the top, she walked over to the line starting to settle down, but some of her emotions must have shown on her face because Dennis took one look and asked her what was wrong.

She gave him a brittle smile. "Nothing. Maybe it's the

fact that I'm hungry," she said in an attempt at a teasing tone.

"I hope so," he said, "because I know you would enjoy this. I made southern fried chicken just for you." Immediately she held out her plate, and he gave her three big pieces.

She laughed and said, "The only thing I'll have room for besides this is some salad." He grabbed a second plate and put a big salad on it.

Seated outside, she felt a little melancholy, wanting to be alone, but not so alone that she was out in the field with the animals. She needed human contact too, and right now it seemed like her contact—limited as it had been—only highlighted how much she had spent every day wondering how quickly she could see Gregory. It wasn't like she didn't treat her other patients with great care, but, in her mind, she was always waiting for an opportunity to see him. She'd just seen him outside, but it hadn't the same effect as seeing him face to face.

There was no longer that same friendliness between them. Something was definitely broken. And, for that, she could blame Dani and Shane. And Meredith also knew that, if she brought it up to them, they would say what really mattered was the fact that Gregory was healing.

So she wouldn't cause any waves because the last thing she wanted was to lose her job and to never see Gregory again.

WAKING UP TO see her standing there, watching him, Gregory took all the strength and determination that he had to not break out in a big smile and reach for her hand. But it wasn't to be, and he'd soon remembered that she'd avoided him for the last couple weeks.

Gregory wanted to go back to his room and get changed, but he could have gone and had dinner with her. He could have spent a few moments in her company, remembering the good things they had enjoyed about each other before. Instead, he let her walk away, wanting it to look like he didn't care. Then again she probably didn't care. So who was he to create something out of nothing?

Angry and fed up and just sad with the whole scenario, he made his way back to his room, where he collapsed on the bed and stared out the window. He wasn't sure what he was supposed to do now.

He was adjusting a little bit more to their workouts. The only good thing about that was how tonight he had lots of energy and didn't need to just crash. The bad thing about that was how he had lots of energy and wouldn't just crash.

It also meant that, once Shane found out, he would change Gregory's program the very next day. According to Shane, they had to continually shift the program and make Gregory's body work to adapt all the time. But he was hungry, and he needed food. Shane had been very clear about that too.

As Gregory changed for dinner, he had to decide on crutches or the wheelchair.

He was still waiting on that prosthetic. He was hoping for it the very next day. He had thought it would be here already, but it wasn't. He grabbed his crutches, put them under his arms and immediately felt his muscles scream.

"So much for that idea," he muttered. *Wheelchair it is.* Gregory laid the crutches against his bed, sat down on the wheelchair and took himself back to the cafeteria for food.

He could smell it from outside the doors. He rolled his way forward to see Dennis's big grin greeting him. "Are you always this happy?" Gregory asked.

"I so am," Dennis said. "What's eating you today?"

"Nothing any different than any other day," he said. "What have you got that'll heal me and get me back up on my feet faster?"

"Well, a plate of veggies and a plate of meat. How's that?"

"Maybe some carbs because I'm tired," he said with a yawn. With three plates, he shook his head as Dennis piled them up with food on the tray on his lap. He made his way down to the cutlery and tried to get some water, but Dennis leaned around the canteen and said, "You go pick out a table, and I'll get you some drinks."

Maneuvering carefully, Gregory made his way to the far end of the deck in the sun. As he unloaded his tray, Dennis arrived with a bottle of water, a cup of coffee and a carton of milk.

"Why the milk?" he asked in surprise.

"Calcium," Dennis replied. "With all that work, you need calcium." And he smiled, moved his empty tray and said, "Enjoy."

Gregory stared at the food and just shook his head. There was enough here for two people, and that just brought him back to remembering Meredith. They'd had every meal together in those first few weeks. Hating the memories, and yet, loving them at the same time, he attacked his steak with more gusto than needed, but, as soon as he popped the first bite in his mouth, he immediately slowed down and moaned in delight. It was tender, tasty and cooked perfectly. After that, finishing his meal was no problem at all. Dennis came around with another bottle of water, motioned at his plate and said, "You only ate half your vegetables."

"I'm working on it," Gregory said with a smile. "But you gave me a lot."

"Should have eaten your vegetables first," he said. "And then the meat. Your body needs the easily digested nutrition."

"It does, so I thought I'd sit here for a bit, then finish eating."

"Good idea," Dennis said. "Don't make me come back and have to pick up leftovers." And he took off again.

Gregory smiled as Dennis walked away. How had everybody here gotten to be so friendly? He knew people at the other center too, but they weren't like this. They weren't invested in his care. Or maybe the truth was they weren't invested in him.

He had thought for sure Meredith was part of the group invested in his healing process, which made her absence these weeks all the more puzzling.

On top of that, she'd been always friendly when he did see her, so it was as if nothing was wrong, as if nothing had ever happened.

But something had, and it was definitely troubling.

Finally, he finished his vegetables, pushed the plate back out of his way and slouched in his wheelchair. His back was killing him. It was definitely time to go back to bed and to stretch out again, but it was sad because the weather was beautiful. A light breeze took away the hot stifling air that he'd noticed earlier, and, if he sat here long enough, the sun would go down, and a beautiful sunset would happen.

Except he'd be watching it alone.

And, at that, he realized how pathetic it was that he'd be

sitting here all alone, staring at the evening. He had to stop mooning over her. She was friendly, professional, and that was it. Their time together was gone, not to mention that who he was before was gone, never to return. It was better he accepted that now and moved on.

On that note, he pulled his wheelchair away from the table, turned and slowly headed to his room for the night. It would be another night hiding away. This time not from physical pain but from emotional pain.

Maybe soon, if he was lucky, he'd finally get over losing her.

Chapter 13

MEREDITH WORKED HARD for the next few days. She hated this arrangement that the others had forced on her, but she would do her part. It felt unnatural, and she felt certain that Gregory would know this wasn't her idea. It was easier to avoid him than to be so professional with him, not to mention it hurt her to see him suffer.

He looked lonely, and at times he looked worse than that. He looked despondent, and she could feel her own anger rising up within. But there was no outlet for her except more work—since she was avoiding the pool now that Gregory had his workouts there—so that's what she did. She dove into work yet again, cleaning up the shelves, getting the backlog of paperwork taken care of. Washing and scrubbing anything and everything to try to keep her mind off him.

On the third day, she sat down at her computer, feeling an edginess sliding through her system. She looked up to see both Dani and Shane frowning at her. Meredith immediately frowned right back. She didn't say anything but waited for them to speak.

"Houston, we have a problem," Shane said in a funny voice.

"What kind of problem is that?" she asked, returning her gaze to the screen.

"He's hit a wall," Shane said bluntly.

Immediately her gaze flew back to him. "Gregory? What kind of wall?" She tried hard to keep the worry out of her voice, but both of them heard it. Meredith could tell from their voices when they next spoke. She sagged back against her chair and said, "What's happening with him?"

"He's gone from anger—which is great, we've gotten rid of most of that—and now he's incredibly depressed," Shane said softly. "And I think that's back to you again."

She raised both hands in frustration. "What do you want from me?" she cried out. "It's hard on me too, you know?"

He nodded. "I know it is. That's why we're here."

She glared at him. "And what exactly are you here for?"

He glanced over at Dani.

Dani picked up the conversation. "We think it's time to stop the enforced separation."

"I see," she said mutinously, perversely not wanting to have anything to do with Gregory just because they said so again. She pinched the bridge of her nose, trying to tell herself to back off and to calm down and that they were looking at it from a perspective she wasn't detached enough to see. "And how am I supposed to do that?"

"Well, you could be friendlier to him," Shane said.

"He needs an explanation," Meredith said quietly. "Otherwise, I'm just blowing hot and cold and hot and cold again. Nobody needs that. Neither him nor me."

"And it's okay to tell him exactly what's happening," Shane said. "Maybe that's what needs to be done so that he understands that you didn't have a choice."

She frowned, picked up a pencil and flipped it end over end between her fingers. She studied the pencil but could only see Gregory's face. "I saw him this morning," she said abruptly. "He looked almost despondent. Depressed."

"Which is why it's time to shift things again. There was this massive well of anger inside him," Dani said. "With that drained out, he's now left with this empty hole. And, with nothing good to fill it, he's filling it with the negative."

Slowly Meredith nodded. "And I guess we have seen that before too, haven't we?" She stared at Dani and then looked at Shane. Both of them nodded. "It's easier from where you guys stand," she complained, though she felt more balanced. "It's hard from here. I'm not detached enough to accept the games you're playing, even though I've participated in them before."

"Which is why it was so important to have you back off initially," Dani said gently.

"And why it's equally important now that you stop backing off and step forward," Shane said.

The two of them stepped out and walked toward the hallway.

Shane called back, "I know it's not something you can turn off and on like that, but sometime today would be good." And the two of them disappeared.

Long after they were gone, she sat here, trying to work, but her mind was consumed with what she was supposed to do now.

She had seen that look on Gregory's face; she had seen that horrible sense of his loss. But she didn't know what was causing that. She highly doubted it was her, but, if it was, then she and Gregory needed to clear the air. Because Shane's words had struck a chord. She had a well of emptiness inside her too. And it had been there for five long years.

At lunchtime, she walked into the cafeteria, her mind still consumed with Gregory. She quickly made herself a salad and went to sit out on the deck. No sign of Gregory.

She dawdled over her salad, watching who came in, her antennae always up and looking for him, of course, but still, she saw no sign of him.

Finally, she finished eating, put away her dishes and headed down the stairs to the pool area, wondering if he was there. But it was empty. Stumped, more than a little upset at the situation and upset at herself for not being able to let it go, she walked out to the animals and wandered around. Off to the far side, a good two hundred yards away, down one of the lonelier stretches of the pathway, was a wheelchair with somebody sitting in it. In her heart of hearts, she knew it would be Gregory.

Frowning, not sure if it was the right time but unable to leave him alone like that, Meredith walked over to make sure it was him. Sure enough, he sat here, staring at the animals.

"I'm surprised to find you here," she said when she got closer.

Startled, he looked up at her, shrugged and said, "It's not like I can leave."

"Ouch," she said with a bright smile. "Maybe not, but I hear you have a prosthetic leg coming pretty quick."

"They've been telling me that for days," he said. "I think it's just a catch-all answer."

"Meaning, you haven't got it yet?"

"No," he said, "and it would be nice to get it. I'd love to walk independently."

"Understood. I'll take a look for it when I get back to the office." She frowned. "If I recall correctly, it should have arrived a week ago."

"That's what Shane said, but sometimes I wonder if Shane is telling the truth." On that note, he gave her a cryptic look, turned his wheelchair around and said, "See you later." And he rolled away from her.

She stood here for a long moment, wondering what else she could have said. But he'd left it kind of cut-and-dried and left her without much to say. She followed behind him at a slower pace and waited until he disappeared before she headed back to her office. As soon as she was there, she checked in with Dani about Gregory's prosthetic.

"It's been delayed twice," Dani said, sighing. "It should have been here already."

"I know that's part of his depression," she said. "He also seems to be either upset or maybe suspicious of Shane right now." She quickly explained the conversation she had with Gregory.

"Probably because of Shane's part in all this," Dani said. "Shane worked him hard in order to get some of that bottled-up emotion out, and no one ever really likes the messenger of bad news."

"I know," Meredith said quietly. "Well, maybe I'll talk to Gregory a little bit later, see how he is."

"I've shifted the roster, so he's back on your list again," Dani said.

"Okay, I'll do a checkup in another hour or so." She started her rounds again, checking on everybody, making sure those who needed medication got it and the rest were either at their appointed sessions or were resting and didn't need anything else.

By the time she got to Gregory—she'd left him for last—it was almost four p.m. She was hoping he was done with his therapy, but she also understood that Shane had tacked on the pool workout some days. She knocked on his door, heard a shout to come in and pushed open the door. He sat on the side of his bed, looking a whole lot worse for the wear. She winced. "Ouch, you look like you're sore today."

He shot her a hard look. "This is nothing. Today is actually a huge improvement over the last few weeks."

"Good," she said with forced cheerfulness. "You're back on my roster, so I'm checking to see if you need anything." She studied his muscles and continued, "I know you may not have been terribly happy with Shane's methods, but your body has really, really developed since you've been here." Meredith sounded enthusiastic, even to her own ears. She walked closer, studying the damage along his back. "Wow," she exclaimed. "That's a huge difference."

"Is there?" he asked, almost with indifference.

"I'll show you." Impulsively she put her pencils and papers down, picked up her tablet, took a picture and showed it to him.

He looked at it and just shrugged.

"Sure, you may not see the difference," she chided, "but here's the before picture." It took her a moment to pull up the before picture that she had in her files from when he'd first arrived and had come with medical photos showing the damage. She put the two of them side by side and held it out to him.

He studied one and then the other, and his eyebrows shot up. "Oh, wow. I feel like I need to frame that."

She nodded. "You do. I think one of the worst things people can do is not take that before picture because then they never have anything to realize how far they've come. You have come so far," she said. "You should be feeling damn proud of yourself."

But his gaze, when he looked at the photos, was hooded. "Maybe. I need to be proud of something I've done. Seems like all I've done the rest of my life is the wrong thing."

That was the opening she needed. "In what way?" He hesitated, but she didn't want to let him off the hook. "Joining the navy was exactly what you wanted to do," she said. "It was your passion. That means it was the right thing to do."

He looked up at her. "Even when I lost out on a wife and a family?"

Her breath caught in the back of her throat, but she nodded slowly. "For that," she said, "even if you're not talking about you and me, I do owe you an apology."

He reared back slightly and looked up at her in surprise.

She nodded. "I was thinking of me at the time. I wasn't thinking of you. I'm not normally selfish, but then I hadn't come up against something that I really, really wanted for myself until I met you. I wanted you, and I didn't want to lose you to the navy again." She continued, "So I'm sorry. I made the wrong decision back then, and I didn't think things through, and I didn't think of your perspective."

He stared at her, shocked.

She winced. "And I understand if that's not what you were trying to talk about, and I'm sorry because I probably shouldn't have brought it up." She snagged up her paperwork, gave him a quick glance and said, "I'll make sure I send you this picture."

And she disappeared. As soon as she bolted out of his room and down the hallway, she felt like a fool. But, at the same time, she felt a cleansing inside. She'd said what she needed to say. Maybe, just maybe, she could finally move on too.

GREGORY STARED IN shock at the doorway where she disappeared. His session today had been harder than normal, forcing him to adapt again. Even when he went to the gym for a workout, sometimes everything went smooth and easy, and the next time it was like moving through molasses, and he could not muster up any energy. Today was one of those days. Seeing her earlier had just made him even more upset, and then finding out he was back on her roster, and she would now be seeing him on a regular basis but only professionally, ... well, that hurt.

But to hear what she had just said? ... He didn't even know what to say. He hadn't been talking about their relationship. He'd been talking about other decisions he'd made in life. But maybe he should have been talking about their relationship. Instead, she had been the one to bring it up, but not in the way he'd expected.

She'd apologized for making the wrong decision, for not understanding his point of view. Well, he'd been exactly the same; he hadn't understood her point of view. He loved to think that she had thought he was something that she really, really wanted for herself. It's the way he'd felt about her too, but he couldn't walk away from his loyalty to country and his career. It was part of who he was, the most honorable part. As he'd stared at his busted-up body and thought what it had done for him, his *this is where I'm at now* body, it hurt that she hadn't even mentioned *now*.

She'd been all about yesterday, the past. And he was hung up on that, hating the fact that everything she'd said had been in the past tense. What he figured they needed to do was let the past go and see if there was anything they had to move forward with. He knew that he wanted a relationship with her, but he wasn't exactly offering her much at this point in time. He didn't even have a career anymore, whereas she was a nurse. And look at this place where she worked; it was fantastic. She lived here, all her meals, everything was taken care of. How could he pull her away from that for a life he couldn't even think about? He stared out the window, feeling his heart wrenching, as he realized that they were better off going their own ways.

Gregory straightened slowly, feeling his body had aged considerably since the injury. He quickly changed into swimming trunks, got back into the wheelchair, wondering where his damn prosthetic leg was, and made it down to the pool.

He locked the wheels, and, without giving himself any chance to think, he dove in again. Tired and moving a whole lot slower than normal, he just kept going, length after length after length. When he finally stopped, he was afraid he'd overdone it. When he tried to pull himself out and fell back into the water, he looked up to find Shane sitting there.

"Feel better?" Shane asked. "Or did you overdo it again?" His face was creased with worry, and his tone said that he knew exactly what Gregory was going through.

"No, I'm fine," Gregory said. "Just sad and grieving. A hope that I had held on to needs to go into the past and stay there."

Shane studied his face for a moment while Gregory wiped the water off and struggled up the ladder to sit on the edge of the pool.

"The thing about the past," Shane said finally, "is that you can't ever bring it into the present. But whatever was in the past, if it was good, there's no need for it to be bad now either. Remember the good and recreate it in the present and make something better out of it."

"Easy for you to say," he said in a harsh voice. "You're whole. You have a career and a future. That was me in the past. It's not who I am now."

"Well, I'm not listening to that bullshit," Shane said. "Because I know the truth. I know that who you are right now is better than I am," he said. "Do you think I don't know how much everybody who comes through this place has been through, whereas me, I haven't been tested like that. I haven't had my body torn apart like you guys. I haven't had to deal with the emotional and psychological damage of what you've been through. I didn't serve my country. I was in school, and I didn't choose to go into the military in any form."

Shane was on a roll. "I've often wondered how I would have fared if I had served. I don't think I would have done well. You are who you are," he said calmly, but his voice was low, so nobody else would hear. "Stop knocking that. You're a damn fine man. And any woman—particularly the one who we both know we're talking about—would be very happy to take you as you are. But you have to reach out and let her know that you care."

"How can I?" Gregory asked. "She basically apologized for our past, but it was a goodbye. It wasn't a *Hey, this is where we're at, and let's see where we can go.* It was an *I'm sorry,* almost like she needed to move on."

Shane shook his head. "No, that's not it at all. She doesn't want to cause you any pain, and we had to pull her away to help you get over the anger eating at you," he said, "and we're the ones who forced her to stay away from you. Now whatever happened today—I don't know what that was—but I can tell you that she spent the last week and a half dealing with her own sense of grief and her own loss and her own anger over what we did. Don't blame her for coming to the wrong conclusion. What you need to do is clear the air, and see where you stand now." And, on that note, he got up and left.

For the second time that day, Gregory stared in shock as someone walked away from him. Meredith didn't have a choice? She had been removed from his care so that he could deal with his own issues? How did that work? Meredith *was* his issue. And obviously, Shane and Dani knew that. It felt weird to think that everybody else was discussing his personal life. But he'd come here specifically to see Meredith, and, of course, he'd gotten so much more in a different way. Still, he really wanted her, but her words had seemed so final today. They were an ending rather than a beginning.

Was Shane right? Was she under the wrong assumption, or was Gregory? Or maybe they both were. Was it all about communication or the lack thereof?

Gregory stared down at his stump, realizing just how much better it did look. She was supposed to check into his prosthetic, and it wouldn't make that much difference—not about getting her back, that is—but it was almost like a symbol of moving on again. With it, he could stand on his own two feet.

It was such a simple sign of progress. Hell, he should have just made himself a peg leg and stuck with it. It was also very indicative of how he felt about himself in this world, that he couldn't stand on his own two feet physically or mentally, spiritually or emotionally.

Thinking to himself, he got back into his wheelchair and made his way to his room, where he changed into dry clothes. He grabbed the crutches and headed to the cafeteria. He stopped at the entranceway, hearing lots of conversations and loud laughter. He'd made a few friends here himself but mostly kept off to the side, isolated. He wanted to blame Meredith, which was hardly fair, yet it seemed like, when he was given a choice, he always went to a table where nobody else was.

Dennis called out to him. "Hey, Gregory, how are you doing?"

He hopped over and gave the ever-friendly man a smile. "Hungry and fed-up with life at the moment."

"Well, we got the cure for what ails you," he said. "How about lasagna and maybe some ribs on the side?"

He looked over at Dennis. "What, no vegetables?"

"Sometimes we need comfort food," Dennis said. "And, if vegetables aren't it for you, they are not going to cut it."

"Thank you," Gregory said. "And you're right. I need comfort food right now. So load me up." They went through the food, getting him a decent plate. Dennis grabbed a tray, filled it up and carried it for him. "You do look tired today," Dennis said.

"Tired, worn-out, fed-up." He nodded and said, "Just one more of those days."

"You'll have a lot of them for a while," Dennis said seriously. "But they will ease as you improve."

"I know," Gregory said. "I just wish I was there already."

Dennis led the way to a table out all on its own.

When Gregory hobbled behind, he said, "Let's change that up."

Dennis turned to him and raised an eyebrow.

A group of men sat off to one side at a table that would easily seat ten. Motioning, Gregory said, "Maybe I shouldn't be quite so antisocial all the time."

Dennis grinned. "Come on. I'll introduce you." He

walked over to the table with the others and said, "Hey, guys. This is Gregory. He could use a little company."

The men all smiled, shook hands and introduced themselves. One man pointed at the table and said, "Lots of room here. Grab a spot."

Gregory sat down and started to eat his dinner. He partially listened in the conversation, but very quickly the men turned their attention to him and started asking him questions. He was surprised at how nice it was to have a conversation with somebody who wasn't concerned about his health or his emotional status, and he thoroughly enjoyed himself. By the time he finally finished his meal, most of the men had gone, and he sat and talked with one guy named Steve.

Steve was almost done at Hathaway House. He had another week to go. Steve asked, "How long do you have?"

"Another couple months, I think," Gregory said. "When I got here, I was pretty cocky, thought I knew how to do this, knew what this was all about." He shook his head, a wry grin on his face. "And then I started working with Shane."

Steve laughed. "Isn't that the truth. We can be as cocky as we want when we get here because we've been through it all before we got here. In truth, we're way behind the curve because Shane is way ahead of the curve, and, for that, we should be damn grateful. But, when you're working with him, when you're in the middle of it all, it's pretty hard to find the energy to be grateful."

Gregory leaned back, looked at Steve and smiled. "And that's the truth I needed to be reminded of," he admitted. "I haven't exactly had the nicest thoughts about him lately."

Steve smirked. "Whatever they do here, they do for your sake. You may not like it. You may not like their methods.

You may not like the hard work right now," he said, "but you will like the end result by the time you take a look at yourself down the road. Has anybody showed you a before and after photo?"

"Meredith did one today," he said. "I was shocked, honestly. I didn't get much of a chance to look at it, but she said she'll send it to me."

"Those photos, they're gold," Steve said. "They've kept me going through so much here. I know a lot of the guys don't put any stock in them, but I do because, if I don't know where I've been, I don't recognize how far I've come." And, on that note, he slapped the table, stood and said, "And now it's time for me to head back to my room. I've got a video conference with my family tonight." With a big grin, he picked up a huge cup of coffee and walked on two prosthetics out of the room.

Gregory chuckled; Steve wore shorts and was completely casual about the fact that he had two mechanical legs. And, if he was so relaxed about it, why the hell was Gregory having such a hard time? Of course, it would be nice if he even got his first prosthetic, and maybe one that would fit. Possibly that was the difference. It was amazing just how far he'd come; Steve was right. Gregory hadn't given enough credit where credit was due. He didn't like Shane's methods, didn't like anything about what they'd done to keep Meredith away, but obviously, it had been good for her too. That distance had given her perspective.

And something about that brought up a wave of anger that he had trouble keeping down. As he sat here, the anger grew and grew. With perfect timing, he saw her arrive for dinner. She walked over to go out on the deck, and he waited until she was seated. Then he hobbled away from his table, headed out onto the deck, stood beside her and, in a low, hard voice, he said, "You had your say, but it's time for me to have mine."

She looked up at him in surprise and said, "I'm sorry. Did I do something to upset you?"

"Yes. I get that you're ready to let go of the past, and I certainly accept whatever apology you think you need for your part in our breakup," he said, "but you have to let me apologize too because I wasn't thinking about you. I wasn't thinking about anything but me, and that wasn't fair either."

She started to smile. "Okay, we both screwed up."

"Back then, yes," he said, taking a deep breath, "we both did. And I think, since I've arrived, we've both screwed up more."

She looked at him, and he could see the hurt in her eyes.

"Shane told me what he asked you to do. He said that Dani took me off your roster and that it wasn't personal on your part. For a long time, I thought it was, and I was really angry," he said. "And I think that's what Shane was trying to do, to make me angry enough to make me blow, to get that emotion out. And now the inside of me feels scraped raw, and I don't really know how to handle it. But, when I'm sitting here thinking about what you said, I'm angry all over again."

"I didn't say that to upset you," she protested.

"No, of course not," he said, his tone almost caustic. "You said it for yourself. I get that you're ready to move on. The problem is, I'm not."

She stared at him in shock.

Gregory nodded and continued, "Now you figure out how to deal with that." And he spun around and crutched out of the cafeteria. When he got to his room, he was grinning because, this time, he felt in control. This time, he felt like he'd done something positive to move his own life forward.

And, damn, that felt good.

Chapter 14

MEREDITH SPENT THE next two days in hiding. She alternated between red with anger and white with fear. She avoided Gregory until she could be calm enough to talk to him. She thought she'd had it all worked out until his words the other day. Even now she didn't really have a reason to back away, except that she felt it was something that she needed to do to regain control.

Finally, Shane stepped into her office and frowned at her.

She frowned right back.

"You need to talk to him," he said, shoving his hands into his jean pockets. "Whatever is going on is holding him back."

"I don't think so," she said calmly. "He pretty much tossed a gambit at me, and I haven't decided if I'm going to pick it up or not."

"Or you've decided already," Shane said with a nod of his head, "but, for whatever reason, whatever he said or did is confusing you."

She took a deep breath. "I haven't talked to him because I don't dare," she said. "I might be glad to go in there and blast him myself."

He grinned. "Maybe that would be better," he said. "Blast away, get it all out in the open. Then you can kiss and make up."

"And yet, I'm not sure kissing and making up is on the agenda," she said, turning her gaze to the computer monitor in front of her. "It's not always that easy."

"No, but I do find we make most things in life more complicated because we don't actually communicate. We leave everything as this big nightmare, instead of clarifying what it was that people were trying to say. But I can't have you hindering his progress, so you best decide what you'll do before I have to step in and make sure that the entire team knows what's going on."

She glared at him. "That's blackmail."

"That's called having a relationship at Hathaway House, where everybody knows everything," he corrected. "I get that you are not quite ready, but I am telling you that you need to get ready faster." And, on that note, he turned and walked off.

She sat here, trying to control her breathing for a long moment, because she didn't know what the hell she was doing. Shane was right about that; she was confused. She was torn, and she cared so damn much that she didn't know how to get over her current situation.

Gregory had said he didn't want to find closure, that he wanted to have a relationship. So why was she arguing? Why was she sitting here, fighting it? All she wanted to do was have him wrap his arms around her and hold her close, like he used to when it felt like it was just the two of them alone in the world, when nobody else could quite understand how special what they had was. And now she didn't understand herself.

"He's right, you know," Dani said quietly as she walked inside. "No, I wasn't trying to listen, but I couldn't help overhearing. Most people don't understand what's going on, but, of course, I do."

"I'm confused," Meredith said, her tone hurt. "I don't even know what to do anymore."

"Well, usually the best way to handle that," Dani said, "is to talk."

"I pretty much said goodbye. Said that I was fine, how he could carry on his life, that I had been able to find some closure."

"Well, I'm sure that pissed him right off." Dani laughed. "Nobody likes to be told that somebody's ready to move on from them."

"He more or less told me that I could be as ready as I want, but he wasn't ready, so I had to deal with it."

"Well, you're not ready either," Dani said smoothly. "Hurt feelings utilize words all the time to gloss over the rough edges and to have nobody else understand exactly what it was that you were trying to say. But the truth of the matter is, you care. You've always cared. He cares. He's always cared. The two of you are at cross-purposes, yet shouldn't be."

Meredith nodded slowly. "It's just so silly."

At that, Dani laughed and laughed. "All relationship stuff usually is. The bottom line is whether you care enough that you want a relationship with this man in the shape he's in, as he is right now. And the issue for him is whether he's prepared to step up and be the man who he can be, and does he love you enough to pursue you in a relationship that will last through the end of time for both of you."

"When you put it that way …" Meredith said, rolling her eyes.

Dani grinned. "A little bit of that wisdom was hard-earned through experience, but that really is the bottom line."

"It's not that easy to get there. I've pretty well ignored him for the last few days."

"Oh, you haven't ignored him at all," Dani said. "You are hyperaware of everything that he does and says. And that makes it even more obvious to the rest of us that you guys need to sort this out."

"Sure," she muttered, "it sounds easy, but ..."

"Most things in life aren't," Dani said. "So why don't you take some time this afternoon? I happen to know he has an extended lunch break because our psychologist had to run into town to help somebody at the hospital, so Gregory is free for that session. You have your lunch hour and the first hour afterward where he is not booked up."

"That's like making an appointment," Meredith said, wrinkling up her face.

"So then, make it a meaningful one," Dani said. "Talk to Dennis. Maybe get a picnic and take Gregory to visit with the animals where there won't be any chance of you guys being overheard and then hash this out. It's really that simple."

But the fear was gripping and choking Meredith.

Dani nodded. "I can see the fear inside you. Every day we watch these men face their fears. Some days they do it well. Some days they don't," Dani said softly. "But we've also seen incredible acts of courage from people who we didn't think had it in them. They stand, step up and face the new challenges. Can you do any less?" And with that prophetic question, Dani turned and walked out.

Meredith sat here at her desk, her face in her hands for a long moment, and then she got up and walked into the kitchen. It was still a little early, but she saw Dennis standing out on the deck, enjoying the late-morning sunshine. She walked over to him. He turned around and gave her a beaming smile, but his smile fell away when he saw her face. "Uh-oh, problems in paradise?"

She gave him a half a smile. "Yes, but I'm hoping to maybe hash out some of the problems."

"What can I do to help?" he asked.

"A picnic lunch for two," she said, "if that's possible."

"For you and Gregory?"

She nodded. "We've been at crosscurrents since he arrived," she said. "It's time to clear the air and see where we stand."

He frowned at her and said, "You don't have to make it sound like a death sentence."

"It's kind of the opposite," she said. "He said he's not ready to walk away."

"But?"

She shrugged. "I guess there's no *but*. I just feel very confused about the whole thing."

"Then go back to the beginning," he said quietly. "Go back to the origin, to the start of it all, and remember what it was that you felt. And, if what you felt back then is the same thing you feel now, only more mature and a longer-lasting kind of emotion, then go with it. What you don't want to do is be a year from now, looking back at this moment, and wishing you'd done more, feeling like you've lost something very, very valuable because you weren't willing to reach out and offer something different."

"That's another way to look at it that I hadn't considered," she admitted.

"Well, think about it. How did you feel this last week

when you couldn't see him?"

She stared out over the pastures. That's what came from working with a tight-knit group. "You heard about that, huh?"

"I did," he said. "Probably most of us did. But we also know you were miserable. Is that how you want to be all the time?"

"But I won't be like that all the time," she argued. "It would be a settled issue."

"And that would make it worse," he said. "Right now, you have an easier time of walking away because you're not really walking away. He's still here, so that's still something that you have an option to proceed with. But, once you make that decision, then it becomes that permanent kind of a thing, and it's very hard to open that door again."

"I know, and I don't even have any real reason for feeling this way."

"Sure, you do," he said. "Your feelings don't need to be validated by anything other than the fact that they exist. What you must do is figure out why they exist and make a decision to move forward or not."

"I really love him, you know?" she said softly. She wrapped her arms around her chest, feeling the chill even though they were out in the sunshine. He reached an arm around her shoulder, hugged her close and said, "And that's the only answer there really is." He stepped away and called out as he left, "I'll have it ready for you at noon. Don't come in through the main part of the cafeteria. Just knock on the door, and I'll give it to you."

"Okay," she said. "Thank you."

He gave her a big grin. "We're going to have a lot of weddings around this place," he said, "and I can't wait." With that, he disappeared.

She walked back to her office and thought about what she was trying to set up, wondering how she would get Gregory's agreement. The easiest way would be to just ask him. And maybe he'd be okay with that too. She had to do her rounds anyway.

Meredith quickly took care of patients and stepped into his room. He had just returned from a session with someone—she hadn't checked her tablet to see who it was. He looked up at her in surprise. She held up her tablet and said, "Checkup time."

Obediently he sat down and let her go through the motions of doing what she had to do every day.

"Are you ready for lunch?" she asked.

"I was planning on it," he said. "I'm feeling a bit stifled inside."

"Well, I have a plan," she said.

"What's that?"

She hesitated.

He looked at her and raised an eyebrow and said, "What's up?"

"We need to talk," she said.

Immediately his smile fell away. He stiffened, nodded and said, "Yes, we do."

"So, meet me at the elevator, maybe in twenty minutes?"

He frowned, considered her face for a long moment, then nodded. "That sounds ominous. Is there some bad news I need to know?"

She gave him half a smile. "I wouldn't do that to you." And she turned and walked away, but her stomach was hurting, and her palms were sweaty. It bothered her that she was making such a big deal out of it all, but she really needed to know where she stood, and she needed to know where he stood because she couldn't do the hot and cold anymore. It was just too devastating and too traumatizing to her sense of well-being.

Meredith finished her work and waited for the last five minutes to go by. It seemed super slow, but she was also terrified that something would happen or somebody would come in and take her away, and she wouldn't be able to meet Gregory.

Finally, she headed to the cafeteria and knocked on the door. Dennis met her there, handed her a large basket and said, "Enjoy."

And he closed the door in her face.

TIME ALONE WAS one thing. Time alone with lonely thoughts was something else altogether. What was she up to? Did he even want to know? Hell yeah, he did. It was killing him. Twenty minutes was nothing, but it was also a lifetime. He went over every possible option and still came up blank.

That had been their relationship so far: clarity followed by confusion. And this was no different. Moodily he sat in his chair and stared out the window, waiting for the time to pass. This trip had brought him so close, and yet, in many ways, he was still so far away from getting what he desperately wanted.

They were friends. Dare he hope they were good friends? But he hadn't told her about his reason for being here at Hathaway House. Would she appreciate hearing it or consider his actions in a negative light?

He knew they couldn't go on like this. Someone, somehow, needed to clear the air between them.

And it might as well be today.

Chapter 15

S HE MET HIM at the elevator on time. He took one look at her and saw the basket in her hands, and his gaze lit with pleasure. But almost immediately the light disappeared from his eyes. "So is this good news or bad news?" he asked again.

"I don't know," she said, "but I figured that, of all things that we needed to do, it was to come to an understanding."

"Agreed." He gave a clipped nod and rolled the wheelchair into the elevator. They went down to the bottom level, and there was Racer, sitting in somebody's arms, just staring outside. He looked at Racer, smiled and said, "I don't get to spend enough time with the animals."

"Once you start the heavy PT regime, it's hard to do everything. It takes about six weeks to get adjusted."

"Well, I should be there then," he said. "Actually it's been longer."

"Well, we've had some setbacks, haven't we?" She headed out and down. He followed her, rolling at her side down to the pasture, and then she remembered something. "Oh, your prosthetic came in," she said.

His face lit up with joy. "So, maybe this afternoon with Shane ..."

"I think so," she said. "That should make your life easier." She took him to a lovely spot, where they could sit and watch the animals and talk in private.

"What will make my life easier," he said, "is solving the problem between you and me. And the problem between you and me goes way back. The thing is, we've both apologized for who we were in the past. But we haven't addressed anything about who we are right now."

She pulled out a small blanket then sat down in a grassy spot. "Do you want to sit there in your wheelchair, or do you want to sit down here?" she asked.

"I want to come down there with you," he said. He locked the wheelchair, stood up on his good leg and made several hops before he finally collapsed on the grass beside her. He sat up, looked around, and said, "This is really nice and private."

"And I figured we needed that."

"Yes," he said, "I agree."

She opened the basket, laid out the small tablecloth and unpacked lunch.

"Wow, Dennis went over and above," Gregory said as he eyed the wine, a couple glasses and what looked like big platters of food.

"Yes," she said. "I think he enjoys things like this."

"I don't imagine he gets too many opportunities."

"No, I'd say mostly when there are problems," she said with a half laugh. Gregory opened the wine, poured her a glass, and handed it to her. She set it gently off to the side as she unwrapped what looked to be croissants stuffed with smoked salmon, also some biscuits and jam, a fresh fruit platter and even some gourmet cheeses. In the warm sunshine, a gentle breeze easing the heat, both of them sat apart, yet both were so aware of each other.

At this point in time, they sat here gently and ate.

"So what do you want to talk about?" he asked, not looking at her.

"Us," she said bluntly.

"Is there an us?" he asked.

"There could be," she said, "but I don't want to be going back and forth. I don't want to be apologizing for what was before. I don't want to even be thinking about what was before."

"Is it that easy?"

"Maybe if we're both determined to move forward, yes," she said quietly. "You're a very different person since you've arrived here." Immediately after she said that, she sensed him withdrawing. She shook her head. "No, I don't mean physically. I mean emotionally."

He looked at her in surprise. She nodded. "Yes, your body's changed. I'm a nurse. That doesn't bother me in the least," she said with a wave of her hand. "I get that, for you, it's huge, and I'm sorry. I'd have done anything I could have to save you from this. But there isn't anything I could have done. There isn't anything I can do other than to help you become the best and strongest that you can be."

She waited for him to say something, but he didn't. She took a bite of her sandwich, washed it down with a drink from one of the bottles of water and said, "Emotionally you're deeper, richer, stronger than I ever thought you would be." At that, she saw his shoulders straighten. She nodded. "Not what you expected me to say, I presume."

He shook his head slowly. "No," he said. "I think we tend to see only the deficiencies in our own selves. We rarely look for the good things."

"When you arrived, you were cocky, arrogant, confident, and I knew that you would take a beating ... because I've seen it happen before. Many arrive here thinking that they can ace their time here. We have those who are closed off from accepting help, and we have those who arrive open and willing to try, and then we have those who are full of themselves. They think that they've already been through rehab, so how hard can it be?"

At that, he snorted. "They haven't met Shane," he muttered.

At that, she laughed out loud. "And you're right there. Shane is a force to be reckoned with. But he runs a hell of a team, and he's the boss. What he says goes, and everybody else toes the line because he's good at what he does."

"As I've come to find out," he said. "If he had said that weeks ago, I may still have been on the disbelieving side of life, but I do believe it now."

"Exactly," she said, "and, in the process, I've learned a lot about who you are inside."

"Is that good or bad?" he asked hesitantly when she didn't speak again.

"Good." She looked over at him and smiled. "I'm also learning a lot about myself."

At that, he frowned at her. It was swift, deep and a bit hard.

She shook her head. "I still like myself," she said, "but I don't like who I was back then."

"I thought we weren't going there."

"Which is why we have to have this talk," she said. "Back then I was shallow, insecure, full of myself and thought too much of myself. I wanted you to leave your love and come be with me and make me your passion instead. And that was wrong. I've already told you that I'm sorry for all that. And then you came to me and said that I wasn't allowed to walk away and that you didn't want to have closure."

"I didn't want there to be closure from us, so you could walk away from what we had," he said. Then he stopped, confused. "That's bringing up the past again, isn't it?"

She nodded. "Which is why we're here," she said in a dry tone. "I would like to state for the record that I admire who you are, and I respect the journey you have traveled, and I'm incredibly heartened by the man I see before me now." She reached across, slid her fingers into his and added, "He's a very different man than the one I knew five years ago. But this one is vastly superior."

His fingers clenched tightly on hers. "This one's damaged," he said, his voice harsh but low. "Have you forgotten that?"

"No, I mentioned it earlier," she said cheerfully. "You're the one who sees the damage. I just see a challenge that you have already aced. I think it's incredible how far you've come and so fast. Shane thinks you've done an unbelievable job. He said that, when you got rid of that anger, there was a hollowed-out space inside though."

"That was where the anger used to be, but that anger filled the void from where *you* used to be," he said. "So, in truth, that void is still there."

She looked at him.

He reached up gently, brushed his thumb across her lips and said, "Unless you'd like to come home again."

Her eyebrows shot up. "Is that where I will be? Is that my home?"

"I don't know," he said, "that's definitely where you belong though."

She smiled and whispered, "Yes, please."

HE REACHED ACROSS and gently kissed her. It was a baby's breath of a kiss, just a gentle stroke of lips on lips, skin against skin, but it was heart against heart and love against love.

"I don't think I've ever had a more lonely five years in my life," he said, "but, when I woke up in the hospital and realized how damaged I was, how broken, it finally came to me how much I'd lost because I knew that you would never accept what I was now."

She opened her mouth, but he pressed a finger against it to stop her from speaking. "No, it's my turn," he said firmly but gently stroked her arm. "I needed to come and see you, see what this place could do for me, so that I might get back on track and be as whole as I possibly could. And, yes, I needed to do it for myself," he said impatiently. "But I also needed to do it to see if anything was left between us."

"Well, that was darn lucky for you that I was here," she said, laughing. But then her smile fell away. "It was a coincidence, wasn't it?" He gave her a secret smile as she shook her head. "There's no way you could have known."

"Couldn't I?" he asked. "Did you keep track of me all these years?"

"Well, I would search for your name every once in a while, but it's not like anything ever came up."

He laughed at that. "True," he said, "often nothing does come up. But, in your case, I had heard about Hathaway House. While on the website, when I was studying the staff, ... guess who's on the team photo page?"

She stared at him in shock and sagged back slightly. "You're right," she said. "I am up there."

He nodded. "And then I had to figure out if you were still single and whether you had anybody permanently in your life. And, of course, I can't tell you how many phone calls I made anonymously, asking if you were the woman I was looking for, saying the one I was seeking was married and had been living in California five years ago."

At that, she laughed. "And, of course, they would have said that, no, I was single."

"Exactly," he said, giving her a fat smile. "And that's what I needed to know."

"Are you saying you came here for me?" she asked in a daze.

"I came here on a hunch and a prayer that maybe, just maybe, you would let me back into your life," he said gently. "Even if I don't deserve it, I want it. I fought for it. I came here, and I've done the damnedest I could to put myself forward. ... Never expecting the progress I've made. Or Shane. Or his plans that kept us apart. But the real goal in all of this was to have you back in my life." He looked at her and smiled almost nervously. "So, what's your answer?"

She teased and asked, "What's the question?"

He held out his hand. "Shall we take that path forward? See who we are to each other now? Take it to the end of the line, hopefully, seventy years down the road when we're both old and gray and shorter, curled up in matching rocking chairs together? And, if we're lucky, making a much better job of it than we have done so far?"

She leaned forward, brushed her lips against his and whispered, "I'd like nothing better. So my answer is yes."

And when he finally wrapped his arms around her and held her close—the Gregory she knew from five years ago now merged with the present-day Gregory—made the moment absolutely perfect.

Epilogue

HEATH HANKERSON HAD fought his surgeon hard to sign off on his transfer to Hathaway House. As he was healing at a tremendous rate, the surgeon had finally been persuaded to let Heath sign on with somebody else, and that had let him take the open bed at Hathaway House.

"I've heard a lot of good things about Hathaway House," Dr. Macklin said. "I'm surprised you got in. But then, the fact that you did means maybe this is where you need to go."

"I think it means exactly that," Heath said in a quiet voice. "I want this opportunity. I've heard some pretty decent things myself."

"A lot of other good rehab centers are around the country though," Dr. Macklin said, as he studied Heath's face with care. "You could probably pick and choose."

"That's exactly it. And I have done exactly that. And I'm choosing Hathaway House."

"In that case, there's nothing more to talk about," the doctor said. "You're progressing well, and I would like to get regular updates. We've done a lot of surgeries, so it'll take quite a bit of time to recover. At this point I have no idea how well you'll do, but I'm hoping for a full recovery."

"I know it's up to me now."

"I'll write up detailed notes for the physio team there to continue the work you've been doing."

"I'd appreciate that," Heath said.

"Wouldn't hurt you to send me an email every once in a while too," Dr. Macklin said. And then he laughed. "I still get emails from patients I treated twenty years ago."

"That's because you care," Heath said with a grin.

"I do. It's not easy. We see people in pretty rough shape when they initially come in. We do the best we can, and sometimes it works, but sometimes it doesn't. At a certain point, the medical technology can only do so much for you. In this case, you've done pretty well though. Now it's up to the physio and to your own will to be better."

Heath nodded, and, just as he slowly moved out of the office, Dr. Macklin called out behind him.

"Do you have a specific reason for going to Hathaway House?"

Heath turned, looked at the doctor, and smiled. "Well, Houston was always home. I don't have any family left, but something is drawing me back there. As for why Hathaway outside of the location ..." He pondered for a moment and then said, "I guess the only answer I really have is just this gut feeling about it."

The doctor looked at him thoughtfully for a long moment, then nodded, and said, "Sometimes, as you know, the gut feeling is all we have to go on. In this case, I think it's an excellent call."

As Heath made his way to the elevator, he hoped the doctor was right. Heath had gone over the Hathaway House website with a fine-tooth comb and had talked to several people that he'd known to get help there. Some had tried to get in and had been refused because no bed had been available in time. On the other hand, a couple guys had come out of their treatment there and had glowing praises.

At the end of the day, all Heath personally had to go on was that gut feeling of his. He could only hope it would work out in his favor this time. He didn't have a whole lot of options left.

This concludes Book 7 of Hathaway House: Gregory.

Read about Heath: Hathaway House, Book 8

Hathaway House: Heath (Book #8)

Welcome to Hathaway House, a heartwarming and sweet military romance series from USA TODAY best-selling author Dale Mayer. Here you'll meet a whole new group of friends, along with a few favorite characters from Heroes for Hire. Instead of action, you'll find emotion. Instead of suspense, you'll find healing. Instead of romance, … oh, wait. … There is romance—of course!

Welcome to Hathaway House. Rehab Center. Safe Haven. Second chance at life and love.

Overjoyed at his transfer to Hathaway House, Heath Jorgenson is anxious to maximize his potential and to get better from the multiple injuries that sidelined him. But rest is necessary for recovery, and Heath's body won't give him any. Even when he buckles under and accepts the need for drugs, his body rejects them. And all the determination in the world won't matter when your own body is working against you.

Just when he's about to give up, respite comes from the unlikeliest of sources. The sound of the cleaning lady slowly and methodically washing the hall floor outside his room lulls him to sleep and allows him to see some of the progress he's desperate for.

Hailee Cisco is grateful for the part-time job of washing floors at Hathaway House. Sure, it isn't glamorous, but it's honest work, and, along with her other job, it's enough to pay the bills—of which Hailee has many. When Dani, the heart of and the partial owner of Hathaway House, offers Hailee a full-time job, Hailee is delighted at the chance to cut back to just one job.

Until she realizes that her change in hours has an unintended impact on Heath's sleep patterns ...

Find Book 8 here!

To find out more visit Dale Mayer's website.

http://smarturl.it/DMSHeath

Author's Note

Thank you for reading Gregory: Hathaway House, Book 7!
If you enjoyed the book, please take a moment and leave a
short review.

Dear reader,

I love to hear from readers, and you can contact me at my
website: www.dalemayer.com or at my Facebook author
page. To be informed of new releases and special offers, sign
up for my newsletter or follow me on BookBub. And if you
are interested in joining Dale Mayer's Reader Group, here is
the Facebook sign up page.
https://smarturl.it/DaleMayerFBGroup

Cheers,
Dale Mayer

Get THREE Free Books Now!

Have you met the SEALS of Honor?

SEALs of Honor Books 1, 2, and 3. Follow the stories of brave, badass warriors who serve their country with honor and love their women to the limits of life and death.

Read Mason, Hawk, and Dane right now for FREE.

Go here and tell me where to send them!
http://smarturl.it/EthanBofB

About the Author

Dale Mayer is a USA Today bestselling author best known for her Psychic Visions and Family Blood Ties series. Her contemporary romances are raw and full of passion and emotion (Second Chances, SKIN), her thrillers will keep you guessing (By Death series), and her romantic comedies will keep you giggling (It's a Dog's Life and Charmin Marvin Romantic Comedy series).

She honors the stories that come to her – and some of them are crazy and break all the rules and cross multiple genres!

To go with her fiction, she also writes nonfiction in many different fields with books available on resume writing, companion gardening and the US mortgage system. She has recently published her Career Essentials Series. All her books are available in print and ebook format.

Connect with Dale Mayer Online

Dale's Website – www.dalemayer.com
Facebook Personal – https://smarturl.it/DaleMayer
Instagram – https://smarturl.it/DaleMayerInstagram
BookBub – https://smarturl.it/DaleMayerBookbub
Facebook Fan Page – https://smarturl.it/DaleMayerFBFanPage
Goodreads – https://smarturl.it/DaleMayerGoodreads

Also by Dale Mayer

Published Adult Books:

Hathaway House
Aaron, Book 1
Brock, Book 2
Cole, Book 3
Denton, Book 4
Elliot, Book 5
Finn, Book 6
Gregory, Book 7
Heath, Book 8

The K9 Files
Ethan, Book 1
Pierce, Book 2
Zane, Book 3
Blaze, Book 4
Lucas, Book 5
Parker, Book 6
Carter, Book 7

Lovely Lethal Gardens
Arsenic in the Azaleas, Book 1
Bones in the Begonias, Book 2
Corpse in the Carnations, Book 3
Daggers in the Dahlias, Book 4
Evidence in the Echinacea, Book 5

Footprints in the Ferns, Book 6
Gun in the Gardenias, Book 7
Handcuffs in the Heather, Book 8

Psychic Vision Series
Tuesday's Child
Hide 'n Go Seek
Maddy's Floor
Garden of Sorrow
Knock Knock...
Rare Find
Eyes to the Soul
Now You See Her
Shattered
Into the Abyss
Seeds of Malice
Eye of the Falcon
Itsy-Bitsy Spider
Unmasked
Deep Beneath
From the Ashes
Psychic Visions Books 1–3
Psychic Visions Books 4–6
Psychic Visions Books 7–9

By Death Series
Touched by Death
Haunted by Death
Chilled by Death
By Death Books 1–3

Broken Protocols – Romantic Comedy Series
Cat's Meow

Cat's Pajamas
Cat's Cradle
Cat's Claus
Broken Protocols 1-4

Broken and... Mending
Skin
Scars
Scales (of Justice)
Broken but... Mending 1-3

Glory
Genesis
Tori
Celeste
Glory Trilogy

Biker Blues
Morgan: Biker Blues, Volume 1
Cash: Biker Blues, Volume 2

SEALs of Honor
Mason: SEALs of Honor, Book 1
Hawk: SEALs of Honor, Book 2
Dane: SEALs of Honor, Book 3
Swede: SEALs of Honor, Book 4
Shadow: SEALs of Honor, Book 5
Cooper: SEALs of Honor, Book 6
Markus: SEALs of Honor, Book 7
Evan: SEALs of Honor, Book 8
Mason's Wish: SEALs of Honor, Book 9
Chase: SEALs of Honor, Book 10
Brett: SEALs of Honor, Book 11

Heroes for Hire

Rory's Rose: Heroes for Hire, Book 12
Brandon's Bliss: Heroes for Hire, Book 13
Liam's Lily: Heroes for Hire, Book 14
North's Nikki: Heroes for Hire, Book 15
Anders's Angel: Heroes for Hire, Book 16
Reyes's Raina: Heroes for Hire, Book 17
Dezi's Diamond: Heroes for Hire, Book 18
Vince's Vixen: Heroes for Hire, Book 19
Ice's Icing: Heroes for Hire, Book 20
Heroes for Hire, Books 1–3
Heroes for Hire, Books 4–6
Heroes for Hire, Books 7–9
Heroes for Hire, Books 10–12
Heroes for Hire, Books 13–15

SEALs of Steel
Badger: SEALs of Steel, Book 1
Erick: SEALs of Steel, Book 2
Cade: SEALs of Steel, Book 3
Talon: SEALs of Steel, Book 4
Laszlo: SEALs of Steel, Book 5
Geir: SEALs of Steel, Book 6
Jager: SEALs of Steel, Book 7
The Final Reveal: SEALs of Steel, Book 8
SEALs of Steel, Books 1–4
SEALs of Steel, Books 5–8
SEALs of Steel, Books 1–8

The Mavericks
Kerrick, Book 1
Griffin, Book 2
Jax, Book 3
Beau, Book 4

Asher, Book 5
Ryker, Book 6
Miles, Book 7
Nico, Book 8
Keane, Book 9
Lennox, Book 10
Gavin, Book 11
Shane, Book 12

Collections
Dare to Be You…
Dare to Love…
Dare to be Strong…
RomanceX3

Standalone Novellas
It's a Dog's Life
Riana's Revenge
Second Chances

Published Young Adult Books:

Family Blood Ties Series
Vampire in Denial
Vampire in Distress
Vampire in Design
Vampire in Deceit
Vampire in Defiance
Vampire in Conflict
Vampire in Chaos
Vampire in Crisis
Vampire in Control
Vampire in Charge

Family Blood Ties Set 1–3
Family Blood Ties Set 1–5
Family Blood Ties Set 4–6
Family Blood Ties Set 7–9
Sian's Solution, A Family Blood Ties Series Prequel
 Novelette

Design series
Dangerous Designs
Deadly Designs
Darkest Designs
Design Series Trilogy

Standalone
In Cassie's Corner
Gem Stone (a Gemma Stone Mystery)
Time Thieves

Published Non-Fiction Books:

Career Essentials
Career Essentials: The Résumé
Career Essentials: The Cover Letter
Career Essentials: The Interview
Career Essentials: 3 in 1